A fierce need to kiss that mouth rose in him.

His arms were around her, holding her tightly clasped against the hard wall of his chest. Cecily registered this fact a moment before she saw the look in his eyes. The next moment, his lips had found hers.

His mouth was cool and sure. He tasted of salt and warmth and of some ineffably wonderful ingredient that caught at her heart. The constant mutter of the ocean, the cries of the gull, even the warmth of the sun died into a stillness broken only by the pounding of her own pulse.

He had not meant to do this, had not meant to kiss her, must not kiss her—warning voices were shouting in his brain, advising him of his folly. . . .

ENCHANTED RENDEZVOUS

Rebecca Ward

FAWCETT CREST • NEW YORK

A Fawcett Crest Book
Published by Ballantine Books
Copyright © 1991 by Maureen Wartski

Library of Congress Catalog Card Number: 91-91982

ISBN 0-449-21986-0

Printed in Canada

First Edition: October 1991

For Shirley Gould and Elisa Falcione

Chapter One

Cecily had never seen such fog. It oozed up from the seaward side of the road, wrapped its gray tentacles about the stretch of Dorset coastline, and obliterated the moon. Even so, the driver of the mail coach continued to press onward.

"Stap me if I ever saw such a fogbank," complained the red-faced solicitor who sat across from Cecily. He drew a silver flask from the folds of his greatcoat and offered it to the clerical gentleman beside him. "Best medicine for your cold on a night like this, Reverend."

"I thank you, Mr. Bowens, but no." The minister, whose name was Tibitt, was small and pursemouthed and had a cold in the head. "I do not hold with taking spirits, even for medicinal purposes," he added primly, "but I agree that the night is vile. Better suited for thatch-gallows, highwaymen, and smugglers than honest folk."

Cecily tightened her hold on the large wicker basket in her lap, and the motherly looking woman seated beside her protested, "Now, sir, isn't the

1

night bad enough without you talking habout 'igh-waymen and all?"

Mr. Bowens took another swig from his flask. "It's the fault of this curst war with the Americans. We're too busy fighting the colonials to deal with criminals at home. But don't fear, Mrs. Horris. The reverend and I will see to it that you and Miss Vervain come to no harm."

Somehow this was not very reassuring. Cecily looked out through the window of the mail coach and saw only blackness. But when Mr. Bowens fell silent, she could hear the angry crash and roar of waves.

"We must be nearing the Widow's Rock," Mrs. Horris exclaimed. "It's a nasty spot, I can tell you. 'Twas so named on haccount of a poor girl what threw 'erself into the sea when 'er man was lost in a storm. They say as 'er ghost walks to this day."

Mr. Tibitt closed his eyes and put his hands together prayerfully. The solicitor took another swig of brandy. Cecily gripped her basket even more tightly but said, "Well, we will soon be at our journey's end, Mrs. Horris. You will be toasting your feet at your son's fire, and I will be with my grand-aunt."

"I'd forgotten about that." Cecily wondered at the odd note in Mrs. Horris's voice but put it down to fatigue. It had been a long, jolting journey on the mail coach, which she had boarded at Brighton, and Cecily's muscles ached. No doubt Mrs. Horris's bones were sore also. "So Lady Marcham's hexpecting you, dearie—I mean, miss?" Mrs. Horris was asking.

"Yes . . . that is, I believe so." Cecily's dark brows puckered in a worried frown as she added, "I sent a letter from Brighton, but I did not hear back."

2

"Fault of the mails," Mr. Bowens interjected. "Her reply was no doubt delayed."

Cecily hoped that this was what had kept her grandaunt from answering her letter. Aloud she asked, "You used to live in Dorset, Mrs. Horris. What is Wickart-on-Sea like?"

"Oh, the village's well enough. A fishing village, it is, though there's some that farm their bit of land. My boy's a fisherman, but my daughter-in-law likes 'er garden."

The mail coach jolted, bouncing its occupants like hot chestnuts in a pan. It then commenced to climb up toward Widow's Rock. To keep her mind off the grisly story she had just heard, Cecily asked, "Can you tell me something about my grandaunt? I have never met her."

"Now, then, why should the likes of me, 'oo used to cook for Lady Maples, meet with the quality?" But Mrs. Horris's laugh sounded nervous. "She's a grand lady, from what my son says. The villagers respect Lady Marcham if they know what's good for them."

At that moment there was a loud, cracking sound close by, and the horses went mad. One moment they were plodding along, and the next they were whickering and pawing the air like crazed creatures. Before the occupants of the mail coach could realize what was happening, the horses had bolted.

Up the fog-shrouded road they went. The coachman shouted frantic commands to no avail. Mrs. Horris clutched Cecily's arm and moaned, "Gawd save us, we're going over the Widow's Rock!"

Mr. Bowens swore loudly and fumbled at the door of the rattling coach. "Do not do that!" Cecily cried. "We must all remain calm and—oh, *no*, Archimedes. Not *now*."

The basket on her lap had begun to move, and

3

now a shaggy head poked out. Above the din of curses, cries, and the pound of horses' hooves, rose the loud caterwaul of an indignant cat.

"Oh, heavens," Mr. Tibitt gibbered. "Shoo—get that beast away from me. Get him away, I say!"

The cat eeled out of the basket, evaded Cecily, jumped first onto Mrs. Horris's lap and then onto Mr. Bowens's head. The solicitor's bellow, as sharp claws dug through his wig and into his scalp, almost eclipsed the sound of hoofbeats outside, but Cecily turned her head in time to see a shadow brush past the window. Next moment, an authoritative voice rang out, and the coach rattled violently as the horses were turned. The coach slowed, gave one massive, creaking jolt, and stopped.

Mrs. Horris was flung on top of Mr. Tibitt, and Cecily was almost crushed by Mr. Bowens, who was catapulted against her. As she tried to disentangle herself, she heard the cleric exclaim, "I feel faint. Air! I must have air—"

"Don't open that door!" Cecily cried.

It was too late. As Tibitt swung open the mail coach door, a compact, furry body hurtled out into the night.

"Archimedes!"

Managing to push Mr. Bowens aside, Cecily fairly tumbled out of the coach. The muddy ground was slippery, and fog pressed so close, she could hardly see the horses. Near the horses stood the coachman, who was offering fervent thanks to someone in a dark riding coat.

"If it wasn't for you, sir, we'd be smashed to bits on them rocks down there," the coachman was saying. "Hinches close to the edge we was. One second more, and it 'ud 'ave been too late for us."

He paused for breath, and the voice Cecily had heard earlier commented, "I thought I heard a shot

4

and wondered what fool would fire a pistol in this muck. Was that what set the horses off?"

"Probably, sir. Nervous on account of the fog, they was. Hanything could 'ave bedoozled them. And if it wasn't for yer honor turning them at the very last second—bless you, sir, I hain't seen nothing like it in all me puff. 'Twas like a miracle, you coming when you did."

The horses snorted and pawed the ground, and Cecily feared that the great nervous beasts might frighten Archimedes. She called to him, but there was no answering meow. "Oh, where are you?" she mourned.

"Is he yours?"

The man had spoken behind her, and Cecily turned so sharply that she slipped in the mud. She would have fallen had not a strong, steadying arm gone around her waist. For a moment Cecily was supported against a man's lean, whipcord-hard body. Then he let her go.

"I'm sorry," her rescuer said. "I didn't mean to frighten you. I wanted to return your cat."

Now that it was no longer cracking with authority, his voice was pleasant, well modulated. Over his free arm hung a wriggling mass of fur. "Oh," she cried, "you have him—he is safe."

Silently he handed the cat to her. As he did so, there was a momentary lessening in the fog about them, and the mail coach lantern caught the glint of a heavy gold ring on his ungloved right hand. It was fashioned like a lion, with the tail forming the band of the ring and disappearing into the lion's mouth.

An unusual ring indeed. She looked up into its owner's face but could make out little except for eyes that looked almost black in the murk.

Earnestly she exclaimed, "Thank you—thank you

5

so much. Both for saving the coach and for catching Archimedes. He is old and quite deaf, but he can run quickly when he wants to. I was afraid he had disappeared into those woods."

She could not actually see him smile, but there was humor in his voice as he replied, "I can't take much credit for rescuing him. Your cat walked right up to me—or I should say, he *staggered*. If I didn't know better, I'd have said that he was bosky."

"He is," Cecily agreed. "I gave him port in his milk at Brighton and once more at Dorchester. I thought port would be safer than laudanum, and he seemed to like it exceedingly."

This time the man did laugh—a warm, friendly sound that made her smile. He started to speak but was interrupted by a shout from the coach. "Stap me, sir," Mr. Bowens was braying, "but that was a brave deed. You have earned my eternal gratitude, sir!"

The solicitor was advancing with his hand outstretched, and both Mrs. Horris and the minister were at his heels. "The wretched coach would have gone over the side of the road in another minute," Bowens continued. "Allow me to shake the hand of a hero, sir—"

"It was nothing," their rescuer interrupted. "I wish you all good evening." Then, lowering his tone he added to Cecily, "I wouldn't feed that cat too much port if I were you. It brings on gout."

Before any of the others could reach him, he strode swiftly to his horse, mounted, and rode away into the fog. Mr. Bowens sucked his teeth. "Now, why did he want to fly off as if the devil himself was at his coattails?" he wondered.

Mr. Tibitt sniffed. "Perhaps the man is one of the infamous 'brethren of the coast.' I have heard that smuggling is rife in these parts."

6

Cecily was indignant. "How can you say that? He saved our lives."

Immediately attention shifted to her and to the shaggy bundle in her arms, and Mr. Tibitt grumbled, "Now I see why I have been sneezing. I always do so when a cat is near me. I loathe the little beasts."

"Well, you don't 'ave to sneeze no more," the coachman interjected. "She hain't taking that hanimal back onto me coach."

Cecily protested, "I assure you that Archimedes will behave himself." Archimedes immediately laid his ears flat back and spat dreadfully. "We are very near to the village and to Marcham Place," she added hastily, "and I will pay extra transport for my cat."

But this worthy only repeated that he was having no animals in his coach. "It's hagainst regulations, that's wot it is. Heither get in by yerself, or be left 'ere with that hanimal."

At this Mrs. Horris rounded on the coachman. "Are you mad or 'eartless, you old bag pudding, you? You can't leave a slip of a girl out 'ere so close to the 'Aunted Wood."

She began to argue fiercely with the coachman, and Cecily, who was trying to repeat that she would pay for Archimedes's fare, could not get a word in edgewise.

"Hoy there, what's all this argle-bargle?"

They had been so involved in their arguments that none of them had seen or heard a curricle approaching. This vehicle now pulled up beside them, and a young man in a fashionable driving coat leaned over the side. "What's all this brangling?" he demanded.

Cecily started to give an account of what had happened but was interrupted by Mr. Tibitt's re-

7

peated sneezing and the coachman's declaration that he wasn't such a Jack Adams as could be forced to take a cat back onto the mail coach. If the young lady wanted to get back on board, she would have to leave the animal behind.

Cecily flared, "Very well, then—I will walk to Marcham Place."

"Hoy!" exclaimed the driver of the curricle. "Marcham Place your direction, ma'am?"

"Indeed it is. I am Cecily Vervain, and Lady Marcham is my grandaunt."

"That so! Beg to introduce myself, Miss Vervain—James Montworthy, at your service. The pater's estate abuts Lady Marcham's. If you wish, I could convey you to Marcham Place in the curricle. Nothing simpler, give you m'word! Your abigail can ride behind with the baggage."

Gratefully Cecily exclaimed, "You are exceedingly kind, sir. I have only the one bag and Archimedes's basket. There is no abigail."

"Quite so. Hoy, coachman, where's the lady's bag? We don't want to stand out here in this muck longer than we need to. Be careful with that, careful!"

Issuing commands and directions, James Montworthy descended from his curricle. In the moment Cecily took to say her good-byes to Mrs. Horris and bundle Archimedes back into his basket, he had watched her bag bestowed, shaken out a blanket to wrap around her feet, and commended the coachman to Hades. "That rackety old rumstick," he wrathfully told Cecily as they drove away. "I should have drawn his claret for wanting to abandon a lady by the side of the road. But what can you expect from the driver of a mail coach?"

"I cannot blame him too much. Archimedes did appear quite suddenly." Memories of her cat's sudden entrance brought a smile, but then she added soberly, "Also, there was a sharp noise—a pistol shot, I believe—that drove the horses mad. If it were not for the brave gentleman who turned them on the edge of the Widow's Rock, we would all of us have been lost."

James Montworthy whistled his astonishment. "Would like to have seen that," he exclaimed. "Man must've had good hands. I wouldn't try controlling a team of mad horses. Not," he added complacently, "that I ain't done a bit of driving myself."

The mist had lifted somewhat, and by the intermittent light of the moon, Cecily noted that her rescuer was possessed of a handsome profile. Moreover, everything from the top of his curly beaver to the heels of polished boots that fit his muscular legs to a fault proclaimed a Corinthian, a top sawyer more suited to racing his friends in his curricle or "playing the squirrel" down London streets than driving through Dorset woods.

That thought led to another. Looking about her at the thick woods through which they were driving, Cecily said, "Mrs. Horris mentioned that these woods were supposed to be haunted."

The young man shrugged disdainfully. "Local humbug, give you m'word on it. Little people and elves and some sort of female specter who's supposed to flap about in a sheet. Anyone who sees her is supposed to cock up his toes. That's Dorset for you."

A heartfelt sigh rippled through the length of Montworthy's frame. "You prefer London," Cecily suggested.

"I wouldn't be here at all if the pater would lend me some rolls of soft," the Corinthian said gloomily. "It's cursed dull, I tell you, ma'am, and the pater's idea of a rattling good time is to fall asleep over his port. Luckily for me, Colonel Howard's a neighbor. Joining his Riders is about the only thing that keeps me sane."

Only people who truly belonged somewhere could allow themselves the luxury of feeling bored. With all her heart Cecily envied Mr. Montworthy's ennui.

"In fact, it might've been one of the colonel's men who frightened the mail coach horses," the young man was continuing. "Don't know for certain, mind you. Dined out tonight myself."

As he spoke, the woods ended abruptly, and scattered moonlight fell on a large stone house surrounded by gardens. "There's Marcham Place now," Montworthy said, pointing with his whip.

The well-lit house was a friendly sight. Perhaps her aunt was expecting her after all. Cecily felt her heart pound with anticipation and nerves as a groom came hurrying to hold the horses' heads.

Montworthy jumped down from the curricle and strode across to help Cecily down. "Permit me to accompany you to the house, ma'am."

She shook her head. "You have been exceedingly kind, and I have kept you long enough. The groom will carry my luggage up for me."

With an air that bespoke much practice in such matters, Montworthy took her extended hand and bent over it. "Glad to be of service, give you m'word. Honored if you'll allow me to call on you while you're visiting Lady Marcham."

God send that she would be there *to* visit, Cecily thought as, hefting Archimedes's basket, she followed the groom who was carrying her bag. There was a steep flight of stairs, and then she was lifting the imposing brass knocker on her grandaunt's front door.

At her first knock the door flew open, and a graying manservant—no doubt Lady Marcham's butler—stared down at Cecily. A bemused look replaced the differential smile that had wreathed his spare countenance, and his "Yes, miss?" was almost a challenge.

Cecily's courage almost shriveled, but she announced firmly, "I am Miss Vervain, Lady Marcham's grandniece. Her ladyship is expecting me."

He looked even more astonished. "Ma'am?"

"I sent a letter a week ago." From the manservant's reaction, this was the first he had heard of it. "Is my grandaunt here?" Cecily insisted. "I should like to speak to her."

The butler seemed to pull himself together. He bowed and said, "Please to come in, Miss Vervain. Her ladyship has retired for the night, but a room shall be readied for you immediately."

Cecily almost despaired. Since no room had been prepared, Lady Marcham had definitely not received her letter. Or perhaps she had repented of an invitation that had been issued—and refused—over a year ago.

She looked about the hall. It was dark there, but what she saw made her realize that her grandaunt was a wealthy woman. Portraits in costly frames lined the walls, marble statues graced the anteroom, and a plushly carpeted staircase led up to the second-floor landing. Perhaps, Cecily thought, Lady Marcham is too fine for a grandniece who is as poor as a church mouse.

But such gloomy thoughts disappeared as a servant girl with red hair and a wealth of freckles on her pert nose came tripping toward her. She dropped a knee and announced, "Me name's Mary, Miss. Mr. Grigg has directed me to make up the fern room for you. If you'll let me have your bag, and the basket, too?"

11

Archimedes poked his head out of the basket and hissed so menacingly that the girl backed away. "He is not used to strangers," Cecily apologized.

The girl looked nervously at the basket and hastily led the way up the carpeted stairs. "It's for sure you've had a long journey, ma'am. I'll light the fire and then see if I can find a bit of tea and toast for you—and a saucer of milk for himself there."

The room into which Cecily was ushered was a pleasant surprise. Unlike the dark and opulent anteroom below, it was a study in shades of green. While Mary lit the fire in the big marble fireplace, Cecily admired watercolor studies of flowers and ferns, apple-green hangings and the viridescent shades of the watered silk sofa and matching armchair. Archimedes apparently also approved of his surroundings, for after emerging stiffly from his basket and sniffing the emerald Aubusson carpet, he displayed his one canine tooth in a yawn and lay down.

But though bone-weary herself, Cecily could not rest. When Mary had gone downstairs to see about the tea, she walked to the window and opened it a little. Through that crack she could smell the raw scent of salt and could hear the muted crash of breakers.

"It is very different from Sussex," she mused. Then, as a soft knock announced Mary's return, she added, "I wish it were daylight so that I could see where I am."

"It will be morning soon enough."

A lady had entered the room. She was tall, slender, and dressed in a moss-green brocaded dressing gown trimmed with swansdown. She had masses of white hair, which had been braided and piled on top of her head, and high cheekbones that gave character to her lovely, almost unlined face. Her smile was charming, but her green eyes were somewhat guarded.

"Lady M-Marcham?" Cecily stammered.

The lady nodded. "And you are my niece's daughter."

She glided forward to embrace her guest, and enfolded by the warm fragrance of verbena, Cecily began to apologize. "I am being a nuisance, Grandaunt. I fear that my coming has disturbed you."

The lady looked rueful. "I do not like this title of grandaunt. It makes me feel as if I am in my dotage. You will call me Aunt Emerald, if you please." She stepped back and searched Cecily's face before adding, "And, no, you are not a nuisance, but I confess that I am surprised, Cecily. Since your refusal a year ago, I have not heard from you."

"I sent you a letter from Sussex last week, but I collect that you might not have received it." Lady Marcham shook her head, and Cecily added unhappily, "I know that I should have waited for a reply, but I could not afford to stay on at the Golden George, and try as I might, I could not find a position that would allow me to keep a cat. I had to leave the Netherbys' quite suddenly, you see."

Instead of reacting to this news, Lady Marcham mused, "You have your father's gray eyes and serious expression, but your black hair and that peach-bloom complexion come from your mother's side. The heart shape of your face reminds me of your grandmother, my dear sister Elizabeth. Now, who are these Netherbys, and why did you have to leave them?"

Cecily blinked at the rapid change of subject. "Because I boxed Giles Netherby's ears when he tried to force himself into my bedroom," she replied frankly. "I was his younger sister's governess, and he thought that gave him special favors from me."

Lady Marcham's green eyes narrowed to emerald slits. "Did you inform Mrs. Netherby about this loose fish?"

"Oh, yes, but she did not believe me." A dangerous sparkle lit Cecily's eyes. "I understand that he had played such tricks with my predecessors also and thought me easy game. I should have kicked him down the stairs instead of merely blackening his eye."

"A great pity," Lady Marcham agreed. She sat down on the sofa and patted the cushions next to her. When Cecily obeyed, she commented, "So. You look like your gentle mother but are proud like your father. You are independent in your thinking as well and wished to make your bread rather than live on the charity of an ancient relative you never met."

Cecily's cheeks flushed, but a wry smile curved her lips. "Alas, ma'am, you have painted my portrait to a fault. Papa always insisted that females should not be weak, clinging creatures."

She swallowed hard and added, "I hope you do not regret inviting me to come to Dorset. If it is in any way inconvenient that I remain here, you must say so—"

Lady Marcham waved a delicately perfumed hand. "Do not talk fustian, pray. I am delighted that you are here, my dear. But I wish I had sent a carriage for you. That any kin of mine should stoop to travel on the mail coach is the outside of enough."

Cecily's relief was so sharp as to bring tears to her eyes. She blinked them back and tried to laugh as she protested, "But my travels were vastly entertaining, ma'am."

She gave her grandaunt a lively account of the evening's adventures. Lady Marcham listened carefully, but when Cecily recounted her dramatic rescue, she paled a little.

"The Widow's Rock is a dangerous place. How foolish of the coachman to press on in spite of fog. As to Colonel Howard, he and his so-called Riders are muttonheads. Why should they bother to hunt for smugglers, when the place is already crawling with excisemen?" For a moment she frowned and then added, "But you are here and safe now, my dear, and Archimedes, too."

At sound of his name, the cat raised his head sleepily, picked himself up from his place by the fire, and strolled over to sniff at Lady Marcham's gown. Then, to Cecily's surprise, he rubbed his shaggy gray head against the lady's knee.

"I am persuaded that he likes you," Cecily exclaimed. "How extraordinary! Archimedes usually loathes strangers, and here he has made two friends in one night. The gentleman with the lion ring said that Archimedes walked directly to him—but that was probably because he was foxed."

Lady Marcham bent to rub the cat's chin. "You mean young James Montworthy? A good-looking boy, but a perfect sapskull. He can think of nothing but hunting and racing curricles and considers himself irresistible to females. No, my dear, I prefer Trevor, though he can be irritating, too."

Seeing that Cecily looked blank, Lady Marcham closed her eyes and shook her head. "I *must* be in my dotage. I forgot to tell you that I have another guest here at Marcham Place. Lord Brandon is the eldest son of the Duke of Pershing. The late duchess was my bosom bow, and so Trevor is my godson."

"Could Lord Brandon have been the gentleman

who rescued us tonight?" Cecily wondered and was surprised when her grandaunt burst out laughing.

"Trevor? Oh, good heavens, no. La, my dear, *what* an idea. When you meet him, you will understand how amusing that is."

But instead of listening, Cecily was staring at her grandaunt's feet. As she had leaned back to laugh, Lady Marcham's dressing gown had slipped up to reveal not bedroom slippers but leather boots. Wet, muddy boots.

Lady Marcham followed her grandniece's eyes. "You have found me out." She sighed ruefully. "You see, Grigg has been with me for so long that he has become a tyrant. He glumps at me if I so much as mention a stroll after dinner, and I should never have heard the end of it if he saw me walking in my garden. It's the best time to gather them, of course."

"To gather what, ma'am?"

Smiling into her niece's bewildered face, Lady Marcham explained, "Herbs. Cecily. Did your papa never tell you that my grandmother was accounted a 'wise woman'? She taught me all she knew about the healing power of plants." She added thoughtfully, "Of course there were some superstitious cabbage-heads who considered Grandmama a witch, but since she was kind and good and—more to the point—rich and powerful, nobody dared to openly accuse her of sorcery."

"How idiotic," Cecily exclaimed.

"That is what I say. But though this is 1814, I am persuaded that a number of want-wit locals are convinced I use bats' tongues and toads' warts in my distillations. But enough of such foolishness. You are exhausted and must rest."

She kissed Cecily, rose to her feet, and in spite of those heavy leather boots, seemed to glide out of

16

the chamber. Archimedes followed her to the door, twitched his lumpy tail, then sat down to gaze at Cecily out of unwinking golden eyes.

Cecily stared back in thoughtful silence. She was remembering the tone of voice in which Mrs. Horris had spoken of Lady Marcham.

"This is extraordinary," she said at last. "Archimedes, it seems that we have got a sorceress for a grandaunt."

Chapter Two

Lullabied by the sound of distant waves, Cecily slept soundly until her dreams were invaded by a persistent meowing. Eyes still closed, she muttered, "Archimedes, pray go back to sleep."

Her only answer was a fiendish howl. Cecily sat straight up in bed and for a moment felt disoriented. Then memory of last night's events came back. She was in the fern room at Marcham Place, and her cat was crouched on the windowsill.

His back was arched, his neck was tensed, and as he stared at some point in the distance, his tail furiously slashed the air. "I collect that you have spied a pigeon," Cecily said in tones of resignation. "You know very well that you are too slow even to catch a snail, and it is too bad of you to frighten me half to death. Now will you—"

The cat interrupted her by slithering through the narrow opening in the window. "Archimedes," Cecily shouted, "come back at once!"

She jumped out of bed and ran to throw open the window. It overlooked Lady Marcham's rose gardens, where, under a cloudy sky, the flowers looked heavy-headed and out of sorts. In the center of the garden was a marble statue of Cupid holding a basin. Birds of every description were feeding from this basin.

Archimedes, belly to the ground and lumpy tail outstretched, was stalking the birds. Cecily leaned her arms on the windowsill and waited until the cat made its spring. As expected, he did not reach the top of the basin and instead tumbled backward into the rosebushes. The birds scattered, and Archimedes gave chase. In a few moments he had disappeared into the japonica bushes that edged the rose garden.

"Drat that cat," Cecily exclaimed.

Archimedes's sense of direction was as faulty as his timing, and he was sure to get lost in these unfamiliar surroundings. Cecily tossed off her nightcap and gown, dressed hastily, barely paused to brush back her hair, then donned stout walking shoes suitable for pursuit.

She met no one in the hall, and at the door a bleary-eyed footman stared at her in midyawn. Ignoring him, Cecily flew outdoors calling, "Archimedes, where have you got to?"

He was not in the rose gardens. Still calling to her cat, Cecily followed a path that led through the japonica bushes into another larger garden where topiary trees edged beds of flowers and greenery. A brass sundial shaped like a sunflower turned its face skyward, and a large marble statue of Ceres presided over the point where the garden opened up into the woods beyond.

From the fragrance that hung over the place, Cecily knew she had found her grandaunt's herb garden. She looked around her, but there was still no sign of Archimedes. "Where are you, you old reprobate?" she cried, exasperated.

"Were you addressin' me?"

Cecily whipped around as a gentleman rose from a marble bench. The bench had been half concealed by the statue of Ceres, so she had not noticed him before, but now that he advanced upon her, she wondered how she could have possibly overlooked him.

Even at this early hour he was dressed in colors that rivaled the flowers. He wore a bottle-green double-breasted jacket with five brass buttons, each as big as a man's fist. The collar of his yellow shirt rose fashionably high upon his cheeks, and there was the glint of gold in the intricate folds of his snowy cravat. His close-fitting, high-waisted pantaloons of canary-yellow stockinette disappeared into glossy high-heeled boots with gold tassels. As he sauntered closer to her, he fumbled with one long-fingered hand at the quizzing glass that hung on a gold riband about his neck.

"Were you addressin' me?" the gentleman repeated.

His voice was both affected and bored. He looked too torpid even to hold up his gold-handled walking stick. Cecily blushed furiously, curtsied and said, "No, indeed, I—that is to say, I apologize for startling you, sir. I was looking for my cat."

"Cat?" The dandified gentleman looked vaguely about. "Don't see any cat, 'pon my honor. Does this feline belong to you, ma'am?"

"I am afraid so. I brought him here with me, and I am persuaded that he will be lost if—there you are!"

The old tomcat had calmly stalked out of the woods. His coat was covered with burrs, his tail had swelled to three times its normal size, and his one tooth pulled his lip up into a sneer.

Lord Brandon lifted his quizzing glass to his eye.

"Animal looks a trifle hagged, 'pon my honor. Is it the same one you've lost, ma'am?"

"Yes. Archimedes, come here," Cecily said. The cat looked the other way. "I am Cecily Vervain, Lady Marcham's grandniece," she continued. "I am sorry to have disturbed you, sir."

As the gentleman bowed, Cecily was sure she heard the whalebone in his corset creaking. "Lord Brandon, at your service, Miss Verving."

Cecily frankly stared. Her late father had been an admirer of the Ice Duke, as Pershing was known in some circles, but nothing of the stern soldier and statesman could she see in his eldest son. It was no wonder, Cecily thought, that Aunt Emerald had laughed at the notion that her godson could have rescued anyone.

She looked critically at the lord, who was of medium height and looked to be in his early thirties. He had an aquiline nose, a strong chin, and a fine mouth and might have been almost handsome if it were not for his affectations and graces. Though he had not gone so far as to paint his face and hands with lead, as many of the London dandies did, he wore a large decorative patch at the corner of his lips and another one near his eye. Cecily could hardly tell the color of those eyes, since they were half-concealed by heavy, drooping eyelids.

Even so, they were taking her measure. Cecily sensed that she was being examined, weighed, judged, and discarded in one lazy blink of those hooded eyelids. "Stayin' in Dorset long, Miss Vervant?" Lord Brandon drawled.

"My name is not—" but Cecily was interrupted by a yelp from Brandon.

"Do you see that?" he demanded.

Was she dealing with a Bedlamite? "What must I see?" Cecily asked cautiously.

"Lint!" Lord Brandon extended his right arm and tapped the immaculate sleeve of his coat. "Look at that—it's lint. Andrews will hear of this. It's intolerable, 'pon my honor. He knows that I insist that all my clothin' be immaculate."

He withdrew his arm, produced a jeweled snuffbox from his pocket, shook a pinch out on his wrist, and inhaled. Every movement he made was in such slow motion that Cecily began to feel sleepy herself.

"If you will excuse me," she said briskly, "I must take my cat back to the house."

But as she started toward him, Archimedes got up and began to walk toward the woods. "Do come here," Cecily pleaded, but the cat paid no attention. "Oh, Archimedes, why are you behaving so badly?"

"I say, cat." Lord Brandon tapped the ground with his stick. "Here, puss. Come here, tabby."

To Cecily's utter astonishment, Archimedes turned, hesitated, then began to saunter toward Lord Brandon. Here he paused and sniffed the lord's natty boots.

"I do not believe it. He *listened* to you. But," she added in some alarm, "I beg that you will not touch him. Archimedes does not like strangers—"

She broke off in astonishment as the cat went belly-up in front of Lord Brandon.

"I grew up with a lot of cats," he explained. "Sensible creatures, I always thought, with a proper feelin' for important things like eatin' and sleepin'."

Languidly he stooped to rub Archimedes's stomach. There was a dull glint of gold, and Cecily started as she saw the ring on Lord Brandon's right ring finger.

"Good Lord," she exclaimed.

The ring that was shaped like a lion swallowing its own tail. No, Cecily thought. *It is impossible.*

22

Her rescuer last night had been a larger man. He had exuded an energy and resolve, and his movements had been full of confidence and authority. His voice had commanded respect, yet had been tinged with humor.

Lord Brandon straightened, withdrew a white lace-edged handkerchief from his pocket, and wiped his hands. A wave of cloying, musky perfume emanated from the handkerchief and wafted across the herb garden.

No, Cecily amended. *Not impossible—ludicrous.*

Archimedes sat up, gave a final approving sniff to Lord Brandon's boots, and began sauntering back toward the house. Lord Brandon used his perfumed handkerchief to smother another yawn.

"You must have arrived late last night, Miss, Verving," he commented. "I did not see you at dinner. It was a very good dinner, 'pon my honor. My godmother has a good cook—a female cook, which is not considered tonnish, but you have to make allowances for the country."

Cecily, her eyes still on the lion ring, could think of nothing to say except, "Aha."

"By now, no doubt, the worthy Mrs. Horrifant has laden the breakfast table with specimens of her art. I'm hungry as a bear, I assure you."

He looked like a very sleepy bear. Even so, Cecily felt she had to make one more effort. "I arrived very late last night," she said. "There was a very thick fog, and the driver of the coach could not go fast. You know what it is to drive in fog."

Lord Brandon looked indignant. "On the contrary, I assure you I don't. Ridin' at night is ruinous to the complexion, especially ridin' in the fog."

Impossible *and* ludicrous. Cecily turned and began to follow Archimedes out of the herb garden.

Lord Brandon fell into step beside her. "Very important, the complexion," he told her earnestly. "It's got to be preserved, Miss Verving, at all costs! I myself use certain herbs, which I personally gather each mornin' fresh from Lady M.'s garden. It's an exhaustin' task, but a man only has one skin."

Had he actually *giggled*? Cecily glanced askance at the strutting figure beside her and mentally shrugged her shoulders. So much for wild imaginings, she thought. If Lord Brandon was in any way heroic, pigs would commence to fly.

Archimedes chose to reenter Marcham House through the window, and Cecily, who had hastened upstairs to prepare for breakfast, found Mary cowering outside her chamber door.

"Holy saints above us, ma'am," the abigail exclaimed, "it's glad I am you're here. Himself tried to scratch me eyes out when I went in to bring you your tea."

Cecily opened the door and nearly stumbled over a gray, shaggy body. Apparently Archimedes had decided to stand guard over the door.

"What is the matter with you?" she scolded. "You are a guest here, sir, not the lord of the manor! I have had quite enough of your starts for one day, and you will let Mary come and go as she pleases."

"Holy saints, ma'am. Does that cat understand the King's English, then?" Mary gasped.

Cecily glared at Archimedes. "He understands enough not to bite the hand that feeds him."

Gingerly Mary entered the room and, muttering under her breath, stepped past the cat. Recognizing an old charm her nurse had used against witchcraft, Cecily smiled. "I assure you that Archimedes is not a witch cat."

Mary looked embarrassed. "Sure, and I don't

mean no disrespect," she murmured, "but it's fey country here. Aren't the Haunted Woods right here on Marcham land? And wasn't that where our master, the holy saints above rest him easy, got thrown from his horse, him who could outride everyone in the country?"

She continued to talk about the woods as she assisted Cecily to dress and arrange her long black hair à la Didion. "They say that the spirits of the Druids walk there," she related, "and that the little people come and dance on moonlit nights." Then, lowering her voice to a whisper, she added, "And on the dark of the moon, the widow's ghost walks. Last one to see her was an exciseman, found stone-dead the next day."

Probably shot by a smuggler, Cecily thought. "Is there much smuggling going on in Dorset?" she asked.

Mary shrugged. "The brethren of the coast have been active here since my great-grandpa's day, ma'am. There's many places to land hereabouts— Robin's Cove and Gull's Nest Inlet, and Eagle's Point. Those excisemen try to catch them, but the brethren are too clever to be caught."

Was her rescuer of last night one of the brethren? Cecily would have liked to ask more questions, but she knew that she could not keep the others waiting. She hurried through the rest of her toilet and was walking down the stairs when she heard her name called.

Lord Brandon was sauntering down the stairs behind her. "I have just finished rakin' Andrews over the coals," he drawled. "A valet of the first water does not allow his employer to appear in a jacket decorated with *lint*. Not done, Miss Verving. Not ton at all."

Cecily was astonished to note that he had

changed his entire costume and was now attired all in blue. He had on a cobalt-blue coat, cut back to form a square, a waistcoat with pale blue stripes, and breeches of the same hue. He wore stockings patterned with blue clocks and shoes that were almost blinding in their polish.

Effete, condescending, redolent with musk and inherited wealth, the duke's son padded down the stairs. Watching him, Cecily found herself tallying the cost of his coat. The realization that this garment would probably feed a family for a month made her look at Lord Brandon with even more disapproval.

"This morning Lady M. is breakfastin' in the periwinkle room," his lordship informed her. "Usually she favors the marigold room. Luckily Andrews discovered the switch at the last moment, or there'd have been the devil to pay."

"I do not understand."

"Every room in the house is named for a flower and is decorated in that blossom's color. I was dressed for the marigold room. 'Pon my honor, it's deucedly inconvenient to change on a moment's notice, especially when a man's as hungry as I am."

Cecily stopped dead in her tracks and stared hard at him. "Do not tell me that you change clothes each time you enter a different room in this house!"

Lord Brandon raised his quizzing glass. His magnified eye regarded her as though she were some interesting species of insect. "Madam," he intoned, "I shudder to think what would happen if I was so unwise as to wear—orange, say—in the fuchsia room. Enough to bring on a bilious attack, 'pon my honor. My friends would think me a proper cake, and I wouldn't blame 'em."

Cecily herself thought several things, but fortunately there was no time to voice her thoughts, for they were entering a room that was furnished in various colors of blue. Everything from the furniture to the draperies and the watercolors on the wall was done in light and dark tones of blue. The sideboard against a wall papered with blue hyacinths was set with several covered dishes. A round table, covered in pale blue lace and set with Limoges china of an azure tint, was set up in the center of the room.

No one was sitting at the table. "Lady M. is not yet with us, I see," Lord Brandon said as he sauntered toward the sideboard. "I assure you she wouldn't want us to stand on ceremony. Now, let me see if I can guess what is here. Kidneys? a brace of grouse cooked to a turn?"

Almost quivering with anticipation, Lord Brandon raised the lids, stared for a moment, then exclaimed in revulsion. "The cursed thing's empty," he cried.

"I know it is." Lady Marcham had glided silently into the room. She wore a large apron tied around the waist of her deep green cambric morning dress and had a smudge of flour on her nose. "All the dishes are empty, I am afraid. We have just lost our cook."

Lord Brandon whipped up his quizzing glass. "What do you mean, lost her?"

Lady Marcham sighed.

"You mean she's left you? But why? Mrs. Horrifant was devoted to you. She spent years in your kitchen."

"Love," Lady Marcham said succinctly, and Lord Brandon professed that he saw no connection between Cupid's darts and a cook who did a bunk before breakfast.

"Didn't she think to give you notice, ma'am?" he demanded.

Instead of answering Lord Brandon, Lady Marcham smiled at Cecily. "Yes, my dear," she said, "I agree with you. Trevor only thinks of his stomach and his clothes. It is a reprehensible trait, and you are right to want to box his ears."

Cecily, whose mind had been indeed forming this scenario, could only stare at her grandaunt, who sank down into a chair and commenced fanning herself with a napkin. "It really is too bad. Apparently Mrs. Horrifant conceived a tendre for Lord Kildyce's butler. Since Kildyce removed to Suffolk, she has been desolate. Then, a letter arrived yesterday, and Grigg surmises that this fellow made Mrs. Horrifant an offer of marriage through the mails."

Just then the gray-haired butler stalked into the room bearing a tureen, which he set down on the sideboard. Lord Brandon hastily uncovered this receptacle and declaimed, "Ah, eggs and kidneys. Just the thing when a man's feelin' faint."

He heaped his plate, brought it to the table, swallowed a mouthful, and promptly choked.

"I am afraid that I have forgotten the art of cooking," Lady Marcham apologized. "Did I put in a pinch too much pepper? Or it might be the nasturtium leaves I added at the last moment. But heart up, Trevor," she added as Lord Brandon turned pale, "I will advertise for another cook immediately."

"But that might take days!"

"My new chambermaid's cousin has done some cooking and can manage plain fare. I was going to send Gwendolyn to the village to bring the woman to Marcham Place, but the foolish girl was too upset. It seems as though Colonel Howard's so-called Riders were racketing about last night and interfered with her brother." Lady Marcham frowned as she continued, "Really, the colonel is becoming too officious by half. His Riders accused Gwendolyn's brother and some other young men of being smugglers."

As if he had not heard one word, Lord Brandon mourned, "Weeks—perhaps *months*. Lady M., we need a cook *now*."

Cecily decided that it was time to intervene. "One of the people I rode down with was a Mrs. Horris. She said that she used to cook for Lady Maples."

Lady Marcham's expression brightened. "Do you know if this good woman is the same Emma Horris who used to live in Wickart-on-Sea?"

Before Cecily could reply, Lord Brandon cried, "Lady M., this is the hand of Providence."

Dramatically he shrouded his plate with his napkin and rose to his feet. "Breakfast is dead, but there is hope for luncheon. Miss Verving, will you lead the expedition in search of Mrs. Horris?"

Ignoring him, Cecily turned to her grandaunt. "I cannot vouch for Mrs. Horris's skill, Aunt Emerald. She only *said* she cooked for Lady Maples."

"If it is the same Emma Horris that I recollect from my salad days, she is a perfectly good cook." Lady Marcham lowered her voice as Lord Brandon left the room and began to call out orders for the trap to be brought around to the door. "I would consider it a favor if you did go with Trevor, my dear. He is bound to make a mull of things if he is left alone, and we *do* need a cook."

"Come, ma'am—come immediately." Showing much more energy than Cecily would have believed possible, Lord Brandon fairly skipped back to the breakfast table, caught Cecily by the elbows, and propelled her into the hall. Within five minutes he had summoned his valet, refused several hats before settling on a curly beaver, and selected a cane that matched his attire. Then, while Cecily was still tying the ribbons of her bonnet, he marched her out of the door toward Lady Marcham's trap.

"Do you drive, ma'am?" he asked. "So much the better. I am not dressed for ridin'. But," he added resolutely, "I am ready to make any sacrifice in order to acquire a cook."

"I collect that a cook is of the same importance as your complexion," Cecily remarked, but her sarcasm was wasted on his lordship, who was engaged in parting the tails of his coat preparatory to taking his seat, smoothing the knees of his breeches, settling his cuffs, and adjusting the lapels of his jacket.

"Now," he said complacently, "we may be off."

"*Thank* you," she murmured.

He flicked his perfumed handkerchief, and the sun glinted on the ring on his hand. Cecily could not help remarking, "You wear an unusual ring, my lord."

He glanced down at his hand. "This? I bought it in Spain."

"So anyone with a ring such as yours must have been in Spain," Cecily mused.

Lord Brandon paused to yawn mightily before replying, "Unless the fellow bought it off someone else—or stole it."

Cecily did not like this last explanation. She was willing to entertain the possibility that her rescuer could have been a smuggler. She would not believe that he was a common footpad.

Unwilling to dwell on this unpleasant thought, she said, "In your haste, my lord, you seem to be forgetting something. Perhaps Mrs. Horris may not want to go into service."

"If Lady M. wants her, she'll come," was the languorous reply. "You may not know it, Miss Verv-

30

ing, but she's known as a wise woman hereabouts. No one will run the risk of antagonizin' her."

He leaned back in the trap and pulled his curly beaver hat over his eyes. The uncharacteristic energy that he had displayed was gone, and he was once again torpid. Cecily soon forgot about him, and as she drove along the road, which skirted the sea and the Widow's Rock before turning inland, her thoughts slipped back to the events of last night. Suddenly the noise of pounding hooves brought her to full attention, and the next moment several mounted men came careening around a corner in the road.

They were galloping directly toward her. Cecily shouted a warning, but the riders were going so fast that they hardly seemed to see her, and she had to turn her horses' heads sharply in order to avoid a collision.

Beside her Lord Brandon stirred awake. "Easy over the pimples, Miss Verving," he said, yawning.

"Do you know who those people are?" Cecily demanded.

Lord Brandon did not bother to lift his beaver from his eyes. "Colonel Howard's followers. You recall that Lady M. did say that they'd been botherin' the housemaid's brother."

"What gives them the right to bother anyone or to endanger people on the road?" The fact that her hands were shaking made Cecily even more indignant. "And who, exactly, is this Colonel Howard?" she asked.

"One of Lady M.'s new neighbors. He's retired from his regiment and as rich as Golden Ball. He loathes civilian life, so he's found somethin' military to do."

Cecily raised her eyebrows. "What could be military about Dorset?"

"Ferretin' out smugglers. I tell you, Miss Vervant, the good colonel makes life excitin' for the bored young fellows who call themselves his Riders. And he's got his tenants on the hop, too. They chase smugglers all up and down the coast."

As Lord Brandon spoke, they turned a sharp corner and came upon the village proper. Wickart-on-Sea was a small but prosperous-looking place shadowed by overhanging trees. It boasted neatly thatched stone houses and small back gardens riotous with late-summer flowers. In front of one of these houses were several horses and one mounted gentleman, whom Cecily recognized as James Montworthy. The band of gold braid around his arm caught the sun as he turned to look inquiringly at the occupants of the trap.

"Servant, ma'am," the Corinthian exclaimed. "What brings you here so early?"

"Breakfast," the duke's son replied. "This lady's Miss Verving—"

"Vervain," Cecily snapped.

"Miss Vervant is Lady M.'s grandniece. She and I are on a mission, 'pon my honor."

He broke off as a young woman backed out of the hut. "I'll 'ave the law on you," she was crying. "Leave my 'usband alone, you slipgibbets. Leave 'im alone, I say!"

As she spoke, two men dressed in workmens' clothes exited from the cottage. They were dragging a third between them. Behind them came Mrs. Horris.

James's handsome face had flushed with excitement. "Ready to confess, Horris?" he demanded.

"Wot's 'e got to confess?" Mrs. Horris demanded. Her gray hair was disheveled, and her round face was quivering with distress. "My son hain't done nofink, sir."

32

Ignoring her, Montworthy said, "Horris, you was seen prowling about Robin's Cove last night. What were you doing there?" There was no answer. "Answer, you damned idiot."

Lord Brandon raised his head and murmured, "Language, old boy. Ladies present."

"Beg pardon, ma'am. Now, Horris, this is your last chance to open your budget. Otherwise, you're going to the colonel for questioning."

At this the young woman began to sob, and Cecily rose in the trap to exclaim, "Mr. Montworthy, what right do you have to take this man anywhere?"

Taking courage from this unexpected support, Mrs. Horris screamed, "You hear that? You let him go, you mawworms, you."

The men holding Cully Horris glanced uncertainly at Montworthy, who scowled. "See here," he was beginning, when he was interrupted by Lord Brandon.

"Miss Verving's right. You can't haul this man away."

"Why can't I? He's a suspected smuggler."

Moving with slow precision, Lord Brandon uncoiled himself from his seat in the trap, descended, and began to stroll toward the captive fisherman. "Cully's no more a smuggler than I am."

Cecily watched doubt enter Montworthy's eyes. "You know this fellow?"

"We were boys together."

Cecily saw a look of contempt flicker in James Montworthy's eyes. "Next," he all but sneered, "you'll tell me you were *friends*."

"But of course we were. Cully and I used to climb the Widow's Rock on a summer's night. Remember how we used to lie in wait for the ghost, Cully?"

A faint grin touched the stocky young fisherman's lips. "I recall, Master Trevor."

"What *I* remember most is those gooseberry tarts you made for us, Mrs. Horris," Lord Brandon continued. His boredom had once again been replaced by enthusiasm, and he bowed so deeply that his corset creaked. "This is too good to be true, 'pon my honor. Here you are, and here we are. You are an angel in our hour of need."

Mrs. Horris looked blank. "N-need, sir?"

"For a cook, ma'am. The old one did a bolt and loped off with a butler. I hope you'll do me the honor of accompanyin' me back to Marcham Place as Lady M.'s new cook."

The red had slowly begun to recede from Mrs. Horris's face. Now she looked ready to faint. "You mean—cook for 'er ladyship?" she gasped. "Ooh, I never could. I'm not near good henough."

"On the contrary, you're vastly qualified. Memories of those gooseberry tarts sustained me through many tryin' times, 'pon my honor. You'll come, won't you, ma'am?"

Mrs. Horris looked helplessly at her son, then murmured an affirmative.

"Wonderful! First rate! Get your things together, ma'am, and Cully will bring you to Marcham Place instanter."

Montworthy growled, "I say, Brandon, you can't walk off with this man. The colonel wants him for questioning."

"And Lady M. wants her cook. Lady M. wouldn't take kindly to your arrestin' her cook's son, Montworthy. She takes care of her people—as do I."

For a moment there had been a note of something very much like command in Brandon's die-away drawl, and Montworthy spoke in a less certain voice. "I don't want to inconvenience Lady Marcham. She's the pater's neighbor, ain't she? But the colonel—"

"Bit of a martinet—thinks he's still followin' the drum. I know all about it." Lord Brandon stepped past Cully Horris's guards and put a hand on the young man's shoulder. "Tell Howard that I'm takin' responsibility for Cully, here. And if he wants to question *me*, he'll know where to find me."

Montworthy looked unconvinced but held his peace. He nodded to the two men who had been holding Cully, and they stepped aside. Lord Brandon smiled and gave the released fisherman's shoulder a pat. "There you are, old fellow," he said.

The genuine friendliness in that gesture contrasted sharply to Montworthy's attitude of noblesse oblige, and Cecily liked Lord Brandon for it. She was wondering whether he might have some redeeming qualities after all, when he spoke again.

"I feel faint with hunger, 'pon my honor," he said with a sigh. "All this excitement is excruciatin' on an empty stomach." He drew out his scented handkerchief, touched it to his forehead. "Don't dawdle, Cully. Get your mother packed. And you, Mrs. Horris, I beg you to hurry to Marcham Place before it is too late for lunch."

Chapter Three

Apparently Lord Brandon had been worn out by his exertions. As soon as he returned to the trap, he leaned back, folded his hands across his waistcoat, and went to sleep.

As Mrs. Horris elected to follow with her son in their horse-drawn cart, Cecily had plenty of time to reflect on her meeting with the colonel's Riders. Her reflections were not pleasant ones. Supposing, Cecily thought, that Colonel Howard captured the stranger with the lion's ring?

Perhaps because they were passing the Widow's Rock, last night's peril seemed very real, and Cecily did not even try to repress a shiver. She had not known how ominous a place this was, with a granite fist jutting over a steep cliff. Below, the pounding sea reflected the slate of the sky. If the carriage had gone over that cliff, it would have meant death on the jagged rocks below.

"Interestin' view, isn't it?" Lord Brandon commented. He had sat up in the trap and was engaged in smoothing the lapels of his coat. "You can't see it from here, but there's an inlet below. I used to go crabbin' there when the tide was out."

Her eyes still on the sullen water, Cecily asked, "Crabbing in such a treacherous place?"

"Well, boys thrive on danger." Lord Brandon's smile was nostalgic as they turned inland to skirt the woods. "We used to play Mohocks in Lady M.'s woods, here, too. Then Cully and I would racket into the village for Mrs. Horris's gooseberry tarts."

Mention of Mrs. Horris's son turned the direction of Cecily's thoughts. "Colonel Howard seems like quite a Captain Hackum," she declared.

"Captain Hackum—'pon my honor, that's a part the good colonel could play." A lazy grin curved Lord Brandon's mouth. "Mind you, the world's a stage with more villains than heroes in it. And knaves and care-for-nobodys and gull-catchers, too. This mornin's business, now, could've been put on at the Asley Amphitheater."

The thought made Cecily smile, but then Lord Brandon added, "I hope Howard leaves Cully alone. It wouldn't do to have Mrs. Horris too upset to do her duty by Lady M. Miss Vervant, do you think there's hope the estimable woman will be installed in time to produce lunch?"

For a few moments he had sounded almost like a normal human being. "I have no idea," Cecily replied shortly.

"My constitution will be quite ruined otherwise." Lord Brandon sighed. "The balance between stomach and man is so delicate that I—but I see that all is not lost. Help is on the way."

They had come within sight of Marcham Place, and Cecily could now see two horses being walked by the grooms. One was a mettlesome gelding and the other a more sedate gray.

"The geldin' belongs to young Montworthy," Lord

Brandon said. As Cecily drove the trap into the courtyard, he added, "He must've had a bruisin' ride to arrive before us."

Cecily felt a sinking in her heart. "Does the gray belong to Colonel Howard?" she asked.

"No, that's Sir Carolus's nag. Young Montworthy's father, you know. He cooks."

Lackadaisically his lordship descended from the trap and strolled over to help Cecily. Before he could even reach halfway, she had stepped smartly down and was asking, "Did you say that this Sir Carolus is a *cook*?"

"He would like that above all things, 'pon my honor. The squire esteems the art of cookin'."

As Lord Brandon spoke, they reached the house, and there Grigg informed them that her ladyship and her guests were in the violet room.

"Lady M. must be restless, the way she keeps moving about," Lord Brandon complained. Then he called, "Andrews!"

A dapper individual with a sun-darkened face and ramrod-straight carriage materialized at his elbow. "M'lud," he murmured.

"Will this coat do for the violet room, Andrews?"

"In my humble opinion, m'lud, yes. Certain shades of lavender and purple go well with blue."

Lord Brandon frowned doubtfully down at his coat. "You wouldn't be bammin' me, Andrews? It's been a tryin' day, 'pon my honor. Not only did I accompany Miss Vervant into the village on a mission of great importance, but I had to prevent Montworthy from being too zealous. Fellow was about to arrest Mrs. Horris's son."

The valet murmured deferentially. "If those sapskulls had upset Mrs. Horris, she mightn't have consented to be Lady M.'s cook. We'd have starved to death, Andrews."

In his own way, Cecily thought, the valet could look as bored as his master. "And where is young Horris now, m'lud?" he murmured in tones of complete disinterest.

"He's bringin' his mother to Marcham Place. Best tell him to keep out of the colonel's way for a time," his lordship continued vaguely. "Go out to sea and catch crabs, or somethin'. Well, well, brush me down, man."

Cecily frankly stared as Andrews produced a brush with long, soft bristles on one side and a sponge coated with some sticky substance on the other. "One side's for brushin', the other's for lint," Lord Brandon explained. "Though I'm not one to ring my own bell, it's my own invention. Prinny has been beggin' me to present him with a copy, so when I return to London, I must look to it."

He was impossible. About to step past him to the violet room, Cecily glanced up and caught Lord Brandon exchanging a glance with his valet. For a fleeting second the hooded eyes were wide open, and Brandon looked neither lazy nor foppish. Then the moment passed. No matter how hard Cecily stared into his countenance, she could find nothing there save the most killing ennui.

Thoughtful, she preceded him into a room decorated in various shades of purple. There were grape-colored silk hangings, a Persian rug woven in hues of lavender, and furniture done up in violet upholstery. Even the marble mantelpiece showed a faint purplish tinge.

James Montworthy had been leaning against this mantel. When he saw Cecily, he straightened and strode across the room to bow to her. "Miss Vervain," he exclaimed. "Your most obedient, ma'am. Our meeting this morning was unfortunate. Hastened here to offer you my homage, give you m'word on it."

Cecily reminded herself that the handsome young Corinthian had rescued her last night. Trying to set aside the unfavorable impression she had formed of the colonel's Riders, she said cordially, "I must thank you again for your assistance, sir."

Montworthy took Cecily's hand and raised it to his lips. "How could any man abandon a lovely lady in distress?" he murmured.

There was the sound of jaws cracking. Glancing out of the corner of her eye, Cecily saw Lord Brandon struggling to conceal a prodigious yawn. "It seems very early for you to be callin', Montworthy," he declaimed in a die-away voice. "Thought you'd still be ridin' about the colonel's business or doin' somethin' equally repulsive."

James ignored the interruption and continued to gaze down at Cecily. "Thoughts of the dangers you had to face kept me awake, ma'am," he said. "Wish I'd been there when those horses did a bolt—"

"Spare us, Montworthy," Lord Brandon cut in. "Lady M. has already told me the tale of Miss Vervant's narrow escape. Extremely fatiguin', I thought it." He perambulated slowly across the room and bowed over his godmother's hand. "I'm glad to report success, ma'am. By now Mrs. Horris must be awaitin' your orders below stairs."

Lady Marcham looked relieved. "I will go and see her at once."

She rose to her feet, and a plump gentleman who had bounced up from a mauve armchair exclaimed, "I congratulate you, dear Lady Marcham. How worried you must have been over this difficult situation."

"And you are reprieved. Now you will not have to descend into the kitchen to prepare rabbit-and-oyster pie." Lady Marcham smiled as she added, "Cecily my dear, let me present you to Sir Carolus Montworthy. Will you be so good as to play hostess?"

She glided to the door, and the plump squire shook his head plaintively. "I cannot get over how Lady Marcham reads one's thoughts. One had *meant* to offer whatever small skill one possesses in the preparation of luncheon, but one never said anything about it."

"Well, you didn't have to, did you?" growled his tall son. "You're always nattering on about sauces and stuffings and venison and hare pie. People are going to think you're hare*brained*, give you m'word on it."

Sir Carolus looked rebuked. "Quite so," he muttered. Then he recovered, pattered across the room, and pressed Cecily's hand. "Your most obedient servant, Miss Vervain. I beg you to excuse my zeal, which springs from one's interest in the culinary arts."

Sir Carolus was a very small gentleman, hardly more than five feet one. His hair had long since departed, leaving only a memory of a fringe about his protuberant ears. Even so, there was kindness in his mild brown eyes, and his smooth face was as guileless as a child's.

"Lady Marcham was explaining the problem of Mrs. Horrifant's departure," he was saying. "Such a tragedy. Had one but known, one would have brought some viands from Montworthy House. There is in the larder at this moment an excellent baked ham with a walnut-and-mushroom stuffing just barely kissed with the liver of a goose—"

He was interrupted by a rude noise from James. "I cannot see what is objectionable about cookery," Sir Carolus said plaintively. "One must *eat*, my boy.

41

Besides, the Roman philosopher Lucullus made his own salads."

"Those old Romans were foreigners, weren't they?" James retorted. "I tell you, Pater, any Englishman who rattles pots and pans has got a leak in his upper works. If you don't care whether you're a laughingstock or not, *I* do."

Sir Carolus looked dashed again but brightened as Lord Brandon inquired, "The goose liver you mentioned, Sir Carolus. Pâté de foie gras, as the Frogs call it—is it ground or chopped?"

As Sir Carolus happily launched into a recipe, James said, "You'll have to forgive the pater, Miss Vervain. He's always been lacking in the brain box."

"I never heard that an interest in cooking indicates a feeble mind," Cecily replied coolly.

"Fact is, the pater gets embarrassing. My late mother couldn't abide him mumbling on about pies and such fribble. She'd give him a sharpish setdown whenever he started, I can tell you! And our cook has given notice that he'll leave if the pater sets one foot in the kitchen." James paused to add gloomily, "Maybe it's because he was born and bred in Dorset. Live here long enough, and your brains turn soft."

"Perhaps that accounts for Colonel Howard's terrorizing the villagers," Cecily suggested, and James looked wounded.

"Ladies don't understand that some things need doing."

"What things, for instance?"

James was somewhat taken aback. He was not used to having females—especially females who had neither rank nor fortune and were of an age that almost rendered them ape leaders—regard him so steadily out of such forthright gray eyes. Had it not been for the fact that Cecily Vervain was the best looking woman he'd seen since his gaming debts had forced him to rusticate in this benighted part of the world, he would have abandoned the idea of flirting with her.

Perhaps a change of approach was needed. Montworthy turned a melting smile on Cecily and bent close to murmur, "Permit me to say, your dress brings out the color of your eyes. Ain't throwing the hatchet, Miss Vervain, when I say you've haunted my dreams."

"Indeed, I am sorry to hear that."

"I don't mean haunted, like that ghost thingummy that's supposed to walk in the wood, mind you. It's just that since you appeared out of the mist last night, couldn't get you out of my mind. Made an indelible impression, give you m'word on it." James's eyes kindled with enthusiasm. "Most ladies'd have been in hysterics meeting up with a dashed smuggler, but not you."

"What's this about smugglers?" a new voice demanded.

"Enter Captain Hackum," Lord Brandon murmured.

Even without Brandon's introduction, Cecily would have recognized Colonel Howard. No one else could have had a voice that was at once harsh and compelling. Then there was the military shortness of his graying hair, the florid, square face set with intolerant protuberant blue eyes, and the sheer size of the man. Six feet and more, broad of chest and shoulder, Colonel Howard looked like a latter-day Goliath of Gath.

"What's this about smugglers?" the colonel repeated as he advanced into the room. He nodded to Sir Carolus and barely acknowledged Lord Brandon before fixing his attention on Cecily. "Mont-

43

worthy," he requested, "be so good as to introduce us."

Looking uncharacteristically meek, the Corinthian obliged. As Cecily curtsied, she noted the three stripes of gold braid on Colonel Howard's right sleeve.

Abruptly he said, "I am told that you are newly come to Dorset and that you are Lady Marcham's niece."

"Are you looking for me?" Lady Marcham had glided back into the room and was regarding the colonel without much enthusiasm. "What unexpected pleasure brings you here, Colonel Howard?"

"I was riding in this direction, and decided to stop and see how you were, Lady Marcham," the colonel replied. "These are unsettled times."

"How kind of you," Lady Marcham murmured. She smiled at her guest, who grinned back, showing white, square teeth. It was plain to Cecily that they shared a cordial dislike of each other.

"I also wished to be acquainted with your niece. I hoped that Miss Vervain would tell me more about her adventures. Village gossip says that she met a smuggler last night."

Lord Brandon groaned. "Been havin' these delusions long, Howard?"

The colonel frowned. "I do not take your meaning, sir."

"I mean that nothin' can happen out of the ordinary but you immediately assume there's a smuggler mixed into it. You'll find the brutes hidin' under your chair next, 'pon my honor."

The colonel's florid skin turned a shade darker, and his brows drew together in a frown. "Do not mock at things you don't understand," he warned. Then, to Cecily he added, "I understand that you had a narrow escape, Miss Vervain. The horses that were pulling the mail coach bolted?"

"They were frightened by a pistol shot," Cecily began.

"You are familiar with firearms?"

The colonel's tone was condescending in the extreme. Cecily was hard put to answer civilly, "My father taught me to hunt and shoot."

The colonel pushed air through his nose. "Teach such things to a lady? I find that difficult to believe."

"I was my parents' only child. Besides, my father believed that men and women have equal capabilities."

Cecily was interrupted by an odd, grating sound. The colonel was laughing. "I'll take my oath that your father was an original. I have a daughter, ma'am, but if I ever let that sheep-brained chit near a pistol, I'd see myself in Bedlam."

"What you are saying," Cecily retorted, "is that a female has no business even knowing that firearms exist."

"I didn't say that, ma'am—*you* did. Now, admit it. Could not the sound you heard have been a signal sent from a lookout on the Widow's Rock? Take your time, ma'am, and give me an accurate account."

The man was odious past bearing. Hot words rushed to Cecily's lips, but before she could utter them, a cool hand clasped hers, and Lady Marcham suggested, "Perhaps James can tell us what happened. I collect that it was he who brought you here last night."

Montworthy was delighted to oblige. As he embroidered the tale, Cecily saw Colonel Howard's eyes take on an almost fanatical glow. "I thought so," he grated. "Obviously the man was a lookout for the smugglers. Why else would he have been skulking about the Widow's Rock at such a time?"

"Amazin' thing," Lord Brandon commented to no one in particular. "Clever fellows, these smugglers, guidin' their ship into the most dangerous waters in Dorset. In the fog, too."

"Only exceptional sailors would make landfall at the Widow's Rock," Sir Carolus agreed, adding, "One has lived in Dorset all one's life, and there has always been talk about smuggling. Talk without substance, for nobody has ever been charged with the crime."

"That is because the local excisemen are fools," the colonel barked. "I do not believe that the smugglers' ship would sail into Widow's Rock, either. My Riders have sighted a ship off Robin's Cove, some miles east of here. The ship flew no colors. What else could that be but a smugglers' vessel?"

Lord Brandon bit back a yawn. "A fisherman, perhaps?"

Ignoring him, the colonel added, "I am certain that the fellow who saved the mail coach must have been on his way to Robin's Cove. Common thieves, all of them—"

Cecily interrupted at this point. "What proof have you?" she asked.

Obviously the colonel was unused to being interrupted by a mere female. "Perhaps you will explain what he was doing there, then?" he asked nastily. "Or perhaps Brandon would be so kind."

His irony was lost on Lord Brandon, who waved a languid hand. "Oh, have it your way, old boy. Not much interested in smugglers anyway. I never came across one, and I don't want to."

The colonel scowled. "That is the sort of talk that I cannot abide," he lectured. "In these troubled times every Englishman must do his duty. What you don't seem to want to face, Brandon, is that England's war with the colonials is sapping the strength of our economy. And the smugglers make things worse."

He paused and a fierce expression glistened in his protuberant eyes. "I am honorably retired from the service of my country, but I will not rest on my laurels. Aided by patriots like Montworthy and my tenants, I will continue to combat the plague of smuggling. If only I could also wage war on the colonials, I would be the happiest man alive."

"England's loss," Lord Brandon commented.

The colonel's scowl deepened further. "Brandon," he gritted, "Montworthy tells me that you interfered with him this morning. I will not stand for this sort of behavior."

"No? What will you do?"

Cold menace filled the colonel's voice as he said, "I will take steps."

Lord Brandon sighed. "I hope it won't come to that, Howard. If it does, I warn you, I intend to choose staves."

The colonel blinked. "Staves?"

"It's a dead bore for the victor of a duel to be forced to fly to the Continent," Lord Brandon continued in an aggrieved tone. "I don't care for the diet myself. Too much starch."

"I have no intention of dueling with you, you fool," the colonel snapped. "I merely asked that you mind your business in future. You interfered with my Riders—"

"Well, Montworthy was interferin' with the cook," Lord Brandon interrupted.

"To hell with you and your cook!" Colonel Howard shouted.

There was a silence broken by Sir Carolus, who,

47

in a shocked voice, reminded the colonel that ladies were present.

"And we have exhausted the subject of smuggling and of duels," Lady Marcham added. She bent a level look on the colonel, who had the grace to look somewhat abashed.

With an obvious effort he said, "I did not intend that outburst. A soldier must always remain in command of himself. I beg your pardon, Lady Marcham."

Lady Marcham bowed her stately head, and after a moment's pause, the colonel continued, "However, there *is* smuggling going on in Dorset, and I mean to put a stop to it. Miss Vervain, will you please tell me what the man who rescued you looked like?"

"I do not know," Cecily replied shortly. "It was too dark for me to see his face."

The colonel frowned. He was sure that this outspoken girl with the coming manners was hiding something.

"Come, Miss Vervain," he insisted, "I don't dispute that the fellow cut a romantic figure. Ladies are fond of romance, are they not? But you must have seen his face."

"Doubtin' the lady's word, are you?" Lord Brandon raised his quizzing glass to stare at the colonel. "Not ton at all, Howard."

"Miss Vervain?" the colonel insisted.

Thoroughly disgusted with the man, Cecily turned away. The colonel reached out a hand as though to stop her, but before he could make contact, the room was assaulted by an odd sound. "Good Lord," James Montworthy exclaimed, "it's a cat."

The colonel turned and found himself confronting a cat such as he had never before seen. Large, scruffy, puff-tailed, and gray, this animal arched its back, exhibited all its claws, and spat.

"Do not try to touch him!" Cecily cried.

But Howard was not in a mood to heed her. He was furious at himself for having let that idle fribble Brandon goad him into losing his temper, and he welcomed an excuse to lash out at something. He reached out to grab the ugly beast by the scruff of its neck.

There was a flash of razor-sharp claws, the sound of ripping cloth, and the colonel found himself staring down at his ruined coat sleeve.

"I pray you will not provoke him further," Cecily pleaded. "He saw you reach out to me and thought you meant me harm, and—Archimedes, no! Get down this instant, sir!"

The cat had leapt up onto a gilt table. The colonel swore loudly and lunged at him, whereupon Archimedes hissed and backed into a bowl of lavender roses. The bowl upended all over Sir Carolus.

"Someone catch that bloody brute!" the colonel bellowed.

Ignoring all of Cecily's commands, Archimedes loped across the room and sprang out of the open window. "Exit cat," Lord Brandon observed.

In the shocked silence that followed, all that could be heard was the dripping of water. Then, everyone moved at once. The colonel ran to the window and stood there shaking his fist after Archimedes. James examined his chief's coat sleeve for signs of blood. Lady Marcham tugged the bell rope in order to summon Grigg, and Cecily snatched up an orchid-colored antimacassar and attempted to dry Sir Carolus.

"The beast is dangerous," the colonel sputtered. "He ought to be shot."

Cecily looked helplessly at her grandaunt, who

said crisply, "Nonsense, Colonel. The animal was merely protecting its mistress. If you remember, you had reached out your hand to detain my grandniece. Archimedes considered that an act of war."

"And from the looks of things he won the engagement," James interjected. Then, intercepting a baleful look from the colonel, he faltered, "Sorry, sir, but the brute has *talons*. Good thing he didn't draw blood, give you m'word."

"He has drawn something more precious than blood."

Reaching out with his walking stick, Lord Brandon hooked three golden hoops that were lying on the ground. "The cat tore off your Riders' braids," he continued pleasantly. "You'd better repair the damage, Howard, and quickly, too. You don't want smugglers to catch you out of uniform."

Chapter Four

"Sage tea for Silas Woodward's nerves and a maceration of comfrey to ease Mrs. Amber's leg ulcer. Was there anything else, my dear?"

Cecily consulted the list in her hand. "There is the yarrow for Sam Waite's stomachache."

"If young Sam would stay away from green apples, he would not need medicine." Lady Marcham placed some leaves into the basket Cecily carried. "Fortunately, I have an infusion of wild yarrow ready."

"Shall I take the medicine to the village this afternoon?" Cecily asked.

"Cully can do it. Mrs. Horris said he planned to bring us a fresh catch of fish this afternoon." Lady Marcham dropped her shears into the pocket of her day dress and remarked, "You are right, of course. The colonel is a bully."

Cecily stared at her grandaunt. "How do you do that?" she cried. "How can you read people's thoughts?"

"La, my dear, you have a very expressive face. I could tell that you were thinking of something unpleasant, and of course, mention of Cully called forth memories of the colonel." Lady Marcham patted her grandniece's cheek. "You see? There is no magic involved. If you study people, they will tell you all about themselves. What have you observed about Trevor, for instance?"

"I have not been studying Lord Brandon," Cecily protested.

"Really? Well, these herbs will do for now, except for some verbena."

Lady Marcham used verbena to create the perfume that she always wore. The plant was also useful when treating problems of liver, kidneys, and digestion. Cecily had learned this and much more in the scant week since she had arrived in Dorset, but herb craft was not all that occupied her mind. As her Aunt Emerald had guessed, she *had* been watching Lord Brandon.

Seemingly unaware of Cecily's interest, he went about his routine of dressing, eating, and sleeping. It seldom varied. In the morning he descended clothed in magnificence color-cued to the breakfast room and did justice to Mrs. Horris's cooking. Afterward he usually fell asleep in his chair.

After his morning nap Lord Brandon changed his attire for the purpose of walking about. That morning Cecily had observed him in a mauve coat of superfine, white corduroy pantaloons, and a lavender hat, which he wore tilted on one side, but on days when there was the slightest hint of rain, he affected a greatcoat with several capes. He would then change again in order to stroll into the herb garden to think (and take another nap, Cecily strongly suspected). Finally he would repair to his room for the grand toilet of the day.

For at dinner Lord Brandon outdid himself. Last night he had appeared in a cambric shirt so fine as to be nearly transparent, a swallow-tail coat with wasp waist and shoulders padded into soaring peaks, black pantaloons, and silk stockings tied with gold tassels. When he moved, the scent of musk floated through the air. When he bowed, the ever-present quizzing glass glinted among the jewels on his chest. His neck cloth had been extraordinary. His nails were polished. He was that laughable figure, a dandy on the strut, a tippy, a bandbox treasure, a Bond Street Beau. Cecily could almost dismiss him as such.

Almost, but not quite. Perhaps it was the memory of that look she had caught passing between him and his valet. Perhaps it was the keen irony of his wit. That wit and the remembered dark flash of eye did not fit the rest of the picture.

But then, Lord Brandon was rich enough to behave like an eccentric if he wished. As she followed Lady Marcham into her stillroom, Cecily reminded herself that she did not have that luxury.

"From the look on your face," Lady Marcham commented, "I collect that you are considering something disagreeable. You are not thinking of that odious family with which you were unwise enough to take service?"

Cecily's wry smile admitted another close hit. "I have been wondering how to earn my living, Aunt Emerald. You have been kindness itself, and I am more grateful than I can tell you. But sooner or later I must decide how to support myself. I do not have a fortune—"

"You do not need a fortune. You have youth and beauty and, above all, a quick mind. It is a pleasure to teach my herb lore to someone with sensitivity and intelligence. It gives me a warm feel in my heart."

Cecily felt a lump rise into her throat. She

reached over to take her grandaunt's hand, whispering, "Thank you. But, Aunt Emerald, I cannot depend on your generosity forever. It is enough that you put up with me at such a time."

Lady Marcham glanced sharply at her grandniece. "What an odd thing to say, child. What can you mean?"

"Just that my coming was so untimely and unexpected. You already had one guest—"

"If you are worrying about Trevor, be sure that he enjoys your company. Why else would the boy have decided to stay in Dorset as long as he has? Now, then, while I prepare the yarrow, will you put away the herbs we gathered this morning?"

Since coming to Dorset, Cecily had grown to love working in her Aunt Emerald's stillroom. It was an airy, peaceful room containing many objects of interest. As she began to dry some of the herbs and decoct the others, she once more admired these treasures.

First there was her great-great-grandmother's beautiful book on herb lore, written and illustrated in that lady's own hand. There were vases and stone jars from all around the world, some full of herbs and others collected simply for their beauty. There were great baskets full of flowers and ferns, lustrous shells from far-off places, fossils etched in stone, and a butterfly suspended in a chunk of amber the size of a man's fist. In the open windows hung crystals, naturally formed and polished, which caught the sun and spun rainbows across the whitewashed walls.

A late summer breeze sent these crystals dancing. Glancing toward the window, Cecily saw that a man on a black stallion had come riding out of the woods.

"What a magnificent horse," she exclaimed.

Walking to the window, she leaned on the sill and watched horse and rider canter across Lady Marcham's estate. They made a handsome picture, for the rider controlled his steed with assurance and powerful grace. Then he turned his head toward the house, and Cecily was shocked to recognize Lord Brandon.

"Why, of course, Trevor can *ride*, my dear," Lady Marcham said, behind her. "He is, after all, Pershing's son. Collect that the duke was the best rider and soldier in England in his day. Trevor was taught how to sit a horse even before he was out of leading strings."

That might be, but neither Lord Brandon's skill nor his proud black stallion fit the image of an idle smatterer. *The image he is at such pains to cultivate,* Cecily reflected.

The thought teased her as she resumed her work, and it was only when she saw her grandaunt looking at her quizzically that she realized she had been asked a question.

"I am sorry," she said contritely. "I have been rainbow chasing, I fear. What did you say?"

"I was about to test your powers of observation," Lady Marcham replied. "What do you think of young Dickinson?"

Cecily glanced at the young underfootman who had just walked past the open stillroom door. He was well built and rather handsome, with blond hair that he kept scrupulously combed and brushed.

"I know that he has not been long at Marcham Place," she said. "Mary told me as much. He seems to be pleasant and eager to please, but—Aunt Emerald, I am not at all good at this."

"You are doing very well. But what?"

"Nothing, except that he knows that he is attractive to females." Cecily thought of James Montworthy as she added, "I am persuaded that such men spend so much time thinking of themselves that they forget about others."

Cecily did not add that she suspected Mary of having formed a tendre for Dickinson. The red-haired abigail had worn a new ribbon on her cap each day that week and had begun to hum Celtic love songs.

"Ah, well, they do say that love makes the world go round," Lady Marcham remarked vaguely.

"What is this about love?"

The new voice was slightly husky and very breathless, and Cecily saw that a tall young woman was standing in the doorway. Her walking-out dress of cream-colored crepe banded with lace was all the mode, but it also emphasized her angular form and thin arms. A poke bonnet of basket willow hid hair that was so fair as to appear white.

Large hazel eyes as timorous as a field mouse's blinked hopefully as she continued, "Grigg said that you were in the stillroom, Lady Marcham. He was going to announce me, but then he was called away to the kitchen—was I too forward? Perhaps I should have waited."

"Of course you should not have waited. You know that you are always welcome here." Lady Marcham glided forward to kiss the young woman's pale cheek. "Cecily, this is Delinda Howard."

After her meeting with the colonel Cecily had assumed that any child of his would have to be a griffin. Yet there was no hardness in Delinda, who smiled shyly and said in her breathless way, "I am so glad to meet you, Miss Vervain. You are a heroine—how exciting to be rescued in such a way, and by an unknown rider, too."

"Did Colonel Howard tell you that I was heroic?"

Cecily could not keep the wry note from her voice, and Delinda looked flustered.

"Oh, no. That is to say, Papa does not confide in me—I cannot blame him, for I am such a goose-cap. Mr. Montworthy told me of your adventure."

A faint blush stained Delinda's cheeks. Her eyes sparkled, and she smiled. For an instant the girl looked almost pretty. Then she ducked her head and murmured, "I fear I have taken too much of your time. I must go now."

"Stay and lunch with us," Lady Marcham invited kindly.

"Oh, I cannot. I was merely in the neighborhood and wished to make Miss Vervain's acquaintance. I could not possibly—oh!"

Cecily followed the direction of Delinda's gaze and saw that the dancing crystals in the window framed a horseman who was cantering toward the house. "It is Mr. Montworthy," the colonel's daughter breathed.

His appearance was hardly a surprise. Since Cecily's arrival, Montworthy had been a frequent visitor at Marcham Place. During those visits he ogled Cecily, brought her bouquets and fruit from his father's gardens, and paid her many compliments. Irked by the Corinthian's assumption that she lived for his attentions, Cecily had done her best to discourage him, but nothing she said even dented the young man's good opinion of himself.

Lady Marcham looked resigned. "Let us receive James in the cowslip room," she said. "Ring for Grigg, Cecily. And, Delinda, stay at least to take some refreshment."

"I—that is, I did not plan—" The colonel's daughter broke off, and Cecily saw that her bosom was rising and falling at an alarming rate.

"Are you feeling unwell?" she asked, anxiously.

Delinda shook her head and hurried to follow Lady Marcham out of the stillroom. She said not another word until they had reached the cowslip room, but as Montworthy strode in, she paled visibly.

The Corinthian did not notice Delinda's agitation. After bowing over Lady Marcham's hand and greeting Delinda, he crossed the room to the window where Cecily stood and leveled a speaking look at her. "I've waited for this hour," he began.

"What hour is that?"

Lord Brandon had sauntered into the cowslip room, and as usual, his appearance was worth noting. He had changed yet again and now sported doeskin breeches and glossy Hessians, with an embroidered yellow waistcoat.

Contemptuously Montworthy looked down his handsome nose. "Been taking a nap, Brandon?"

"Wish I was," the duke's son replied. "It's been an exhaustin' mornin'. My fool of a groom said that my horse needed exercisin', so I took Ebony through his paces."

Try as she would, Cecily could not equate the skilled rider she had seen earlier with the dandy before her. "We saw you galloping through the meadow," she began.

Hooded eyes turned sleepily toward her. "The brute ran off with me," his lordship complained. "I don't feel at all the thing, 'pon my honor, I don't. I was dragged over hill and dale."

"When Aunt Emerald and I saw you," Cecily persisted, "you looked very much in control of your horse."

"I assure you, Miss Vervant, I was in great distress."

He began to perambulate toward a chair, but Montworthy stopped him. "I say, Brandon, I'll admit you've got a fine brute in that stallion. Carries a good head, and his quarters are well let down. But I'll lay you a monkey that he can't take my Hannibal in a race."

"Of course, dear boy, if you say so," was the equable reply.

Montworthy blinked. In a somewhat dampened voice he queried, "But don't you want to race him—prove which is faster?"

"You already said your animal was faster, didn't you? 'Pon my honor, Montworthy, I wish you'd make up your mind. This ditherin' about is fatiguin'."

Slowly, like an accordion folding, Lord Brandon sank into a buttercup-yellow armchair. "Lady M., is it too much to ask that you ring for a small refreshment before luncheon? Gooseberry tarts, Mrs. Horris was bakin' this mornin'. The smell alone transported me to the gates of heaven."

He kissed his fingers, and Montworthy gave a disgusted snort. "All you can think of is food and clothes. There's other things in the world, give you m'word."

"Like smugglers, you mean?" drawled Lord Brandon.

"Mr. Montworthy is correct." Like a child about to recite a lesson, Delinda sat up very straight in her chair and folded her hands in her lap. "It is well known that the Dorset coast is swarming with smugglers bringing in contraband. These wicked men are undermining the economy at a time when England needs to combat the colonials in America. Anyone caught smuggling or aiding the smugglers is worse than a lawbreaker. He is a traitor to the crown."

"Well said!" Montworthy exclaimed.

Flushing, Delinda murmured, "Oh, Mr. Montworthy, you are so kind, actually, it was Papa who turned the phrase—he feels so strongly that we should crush the colonials once and for all, that weak-kneed politicians are traitors. He has no use for peers like the Duke of Pershing, who counsels peace—"

She broke off, glanced at Lord Brandon, and turned a fiery crimson. "I am so sorry," she murmured. "I should not have said—I beg your pardon. I must leave, now."

She got to her feet so swiftly that she upset a small table and a porcelain figure of a yellow dog. In a soothing tone Lady Marcham said, "La, Delinda, do not refine on it. Differences of opinion are what make the world interesting. If you stuffed a pork roast with only one herb, would you have an interesting dish? No, indeed."

"Pork roast—oh, Lord, I almost forgot." James withdrew an envelope from his breast pocket. "It's from the pater," he said. "An invitation."

Though he spoke to Lady Marcham, his eyes were on Cecily. Noting that Delinda's eyes were sad, Cecily wondered if the Corinthian was completely insensitive or merely thick.

She concentrated on her grandaunt, who had slit the envelope and was reading the contents. "Sir Carolus has been kind enough to ask us to attend a dinner party at the end of this week," Lady Marcham said. "He says here that he is anxious to try a new recipe: a pork roast in new milk."

"There'll be dancing, too." Montworthy looked meaningfully at Cecily. "Not like London, but a country hop's better than nothing."

"I do love to dance," Delinda said wistfully.

Montworthy did not hear her. He was saying smugly, "I'll look forward to the honor of a waltz, Miss Vervain."

Both thick *and* insufferable. But before Cecily

could think of a proper set-down for him, Lord Brandon lifted a hand. "Stop, Montworthy. What colors predominate in your drawin' room?"

"My—how the devil should I know? Green, I suppose. Or blue. What do you want to know for?"

"By now you should know that I refuse to enter a room with which my costume would clash," Lord Brandon replied gravely. "Blue or green is possible. Yellow is allowable. But should your walls and draperies be maroon—Well, well, Andrews will find out for me. He always does."

Andrews reported that Sir Carolus's drawing room was decorated in tones of silver, a color that was deemed acceptable by his lordship. Consequently, on the evening of Sir Carolus's party Lord Brandon appeared in a gray swallow-tailed coat, a shirt of dazzling white with frills, gray breeches, and white silk stockings that disappeared into high-heeled black shoes with silver buckles.

"I wanted to wear gray pumps," he confided to Cecily as they awaited Lady Marcham in the ground-floor anteroom, "But Andrews was against it. He was really adamant about it, so I let him have his way."

He paused and raised his quizzing glass. "You are very fine tonight, Miss Verving. That shade of ivory emphasizes the cream and roses of your cheeks and turns your eyes to silver. Most becomin', 'pon my honor."

From any other gentleman this would have been a compliment. Lord Brandon spoke the words with dispassionate interest.

"Your hair is exquisite, too," he continued judiciously. "I am gratified to see you didn't torture it by crimpin' it into one of the popular styles. A pity that you needed to confine it into that chignon, however. Hair like yours should be allowed to flow free—like a dark waterfall."

As he spoke, he reached out to tuck a strand of hair behind her ear. The words, the gesture, were so at variance with his stilted speech that Cecily stared in astonishment. Then he raised a hand to hide a yawn.

"A curl had fallen upon your cheek," he explained. "Charmin', of course, but it spoiled perfection."

She could still feel his fingers against her skin. Assured and cool, they had seemed to pulse with an inner fire. With some difficulty Cecily shrugged aside such imbecilic imaginings and replied, "I am not fond of perfection, Lord Brandon. It is cold and haughty."

"Who is cold and haughty?" Lady Marcham asked. She had just appeared on the stairs and looked magnificent in her green silk slip with its overdress of silver gauze. Emeralds and diamonds glistened at her neck and in her ears and on her fingers and in her crown of silver hair.

Cecily clapped her hands together in admiration, and Lord Brandon bowed with languid grace. "Madam Godmother, you look the way a queen would *want* to look."

As he escorted them toward the waiting barouche, he regaled them with amusing stories about royalty with whom he was apparently on good terms. In his languid fashion he kept the ladies entertained while the coach followed the sea road, circled Lady Marcham's woods, and then rattled inland across the meadows to Montworthy House.

Though not overlarge, Montworthy House was a handsome property. Sir Carolus's ancestor had built his home in the time of the Tudors, and at that time it must have been an austere and rather formidable place. Now, under the squire's hand, it had changed its character. The front of the house was set off with roses and friendly summer flowers, and a large kitchen garden could be glimpsed in the back.

Sir Carolus himself came trotting down the stairs to greet them at the door. "Dear Lady Marcham," he chirruped, "I am honored to see you. Miss Vervain, your most obedient. Lord Brandon, one makes bold to say that you will not be disappointed tonight. Together with the pork roast in new milk, there will be a mushroom pasty cooked with onions and cream."

"Your creation, Sir Carolus?" Lady Marcham smiled.

"Alas, no. One wished to assist in its preparation, but the cook would not allow it." The little squire sighed deeply. "One must expect disappointments in life."

He escorted them up a curved staircase and into a foyer where an orchestra was playing for the pleasure of the arriving guests. "We shall have dancing later," Sir Carolus explained diffidently. "One feels too old for such pastimes, but James insists that a party without dancing is like lamb without the mint. Ah, here is the drawing room. Will you come this way?"

As Cecily started to follow her Aunt Emerald, Brandon slid an arm through hers. "Don't," he said.

She turned to look wonderingly at him, and he nodded to a thin matron in a plum-colored dress and matching turban. "See that female bearin' down on Lady M.? That's Lady Breek. She's a gabble-monger who clacks away like a Spanish dancer's castanets. Listenin' to her is almost as bad as dancin'."

"I collect that you do not dance."

Lord Brandon looked pained. "Pershing insisted

we learn, and it was worse than learnin' to ride. Dancin' is an exhaustin' pastime, 'pon my honor. What do you think, Miss Verving?"

Before Cecily could reply, a loud male voice exclaimed, "I tell you this. If those rebels don't watch themselves, they'll soon be dancing to another tune."

Lord Brandon winced visibly at Montworthy's declaration, and Cecily glanced askance at a group of young men nearby. All of them, except for an officer in scarlet regimentals, wore gold braid on their sleeves.

"The colonel's Riders," Lord Brandon sighed. "We are caught between the devil and the dark blue sea."

Cecily glanced hopefully toward Lady Marcham and noted that she and Lady Breek were deep in conversation. At least Lady Breek was doing the talking, and Aunt Emerald's eyes had become glassy as she listened.

Montworthy was declaiming, "It's as Colonel Howard says. We're a great nation. Damn it, Jermayne, we can easily crush America."

Beside Cecily, Lord Brandon stiffened. He looked hard at the officer in regimentals, who was protesting, "Not that easy to fight a whole nation. By Jove, no. You'd have to hire mercenaries. It'll beggar the treasury."

A chorus of disclaimers rose at once. The officer shrugged and turned away, and Cecily caught a glimpse of a sun-darkened face with a puckered scar seaming one cheek.

She had no time to observe more before Lord Brandon caught her by the elbow and began to propel her in the direction of some French windows. "What are you doing?" she asked indignantly.

"You were wonderin' how to escape all those tiresome people, weren't you?" his lordship demanded.

There was surprising strength in Lord Brandon's arm, and Cecily was swept effortlessly forward. Knowing that to resist would cause a scene, she allowed herself to be walked through some French windows onto a balcony. As soon as they were alone, she rounded on him.

"Of all the rag-mannered tricks," she exclaimed. "I did not ask to be brought here, sir."

"No, but you'll have to admit it's more pleasant than in there," Brandon drawled.

About to sweep back into the drawing room, Cecily felt a breeze laden with the scent of roses and honeysuckle touch her cheek. She could not resist pausing to glance over her shoulder and saw that the balcony overlooked Sir Carolus's gardens.

It *was* much more pleasant there, but the forms had to be observed. "I must go in," Cecily said.

"Why?" Lord Brandon wanted to know.

Cecily started to speak, then stopped as Lord Brandon continued. "Don't let customs dictate your behavior. Think for yourself."

In spite of herself Cecily could not help smiling. "My father used to say that. He said that manners change but truth stays constant." She leaned forward, so that her elbows rested on the marble edge of the balcony. "He warned me that if I did not think independently, I could never be a free woman."

"Then he was a clear-thinking man, a rarity in any age."

Was it a trick of her imagination, or had Lord Brandon's voice changed somehow? Cecily glanced at the man beside her, but his face was in shadow.

"No wonder you are the kind of woman you are," he continued.

"I do not think—" Cecily began, but he silenced her.

"You *do* think. That is what I find so delightful about you."

This was not a proper conversation. Cecily knew that she should end it, put Lord Brandon in his place, and return to the others. Instead, she heard herself say, "Others do not share your view. I am persuaded that Colonel Howard cannot credit that a female has two thoughts to rub together, and there are many more like him in the world."

"If you could create your own world, what would it be like?" Dimly Cecily realized that Lord Brandon was also leaning against the edge of the balcony. He was so near that his coat sleeve brushed her bare arm as he said, "Come, pretend with me that we are a universe away from anyone else."

With a jolt of consternation, Cecily realized that she had been thinking that same thing. Sir Carolus's guests had disappeared. Annoying memories of Colonel Howard and James Montworthy had become unimportant. All that remained was the flower-drenched night and the man by her side.

"We must rejoin the others." She had meant to say the words firmly, but they came out in a hen-hearted whisper.

Brandon could feel her arm tremble against his, and when he turned to look down at her, he could discern the uncertain look in her eyes. The curve of her mouth made her appear vulnerable, and a fierce need to kiss that mouth rose in him. Though he reminded himself of the reason that had brought him to Dorset, his logic seemed to have taken French leave. In this magical instant nothing mattered more to Brandon than this girl beside him with moon-silver in her eyes.

She *must* rejoin the others. Cecily had half turned

to go when she heard Lord Brandon say, "Don't go, Celia."

Her startled eyes flew up to meet his, and at the look in his eyes her heart seemed to pause. It was incredible—impossible—that she wanted the effete Lord Brandon to kiss her, but this man did not seem to be Lord Brandon. It was as though a stranger, and yet not a stranger, stood beside her in the rose-scented night. When he took her hand, Cecily did not have the strength of mind to pull away.

"Celia," Lord Brandon murmured.

Just then, a shadowy form came striding out of the French windows. It stopped short, and a startled male voice exclaimed, "Is someone else out here?"

Chapter Five

Letting go of Cecily's hand, Lord Brandon took several steps backward and collided painfully with the marble rail of the balcony. Meanwhile the intruder was apologizing, "Only wanted to blow a cloud. Talk in there's as moldy as old cheese. No wish to disturb anybody. By Jove, no."

"You are not disturbin' us," Lord Brandon replied. "This lady felt faint and was takin' the air. If you're feelin' restored, ma'am, shall we go in?"

He offered Cecily his arm, but before she could take it, the newcomer exclaimed, "It *is* you, Brandon!"

He seized Lord Brandon's hand and began to pump it forcefully. "Thought so earlier but wasn't sure. What are you doing here in Dorset?"

"I could ask you the same thing, Jermayne. I thought you were in Portugal."

"Furlough, old man." By a shaft of light that filtered through the open French windows, Cecily could see that the newcomer was tall and had a long face bisected by a drooping, sandy mustache.

The scar on his cheek stood out starkly against his sun-darkened skin.

"Boney's quiet for the time being," he continued, "so I'm rusticating." He paused, coughed behind his fist, and made a jerky bow in Cecily's direction. "Servant, ma'am," he said shyly. "Didn't mean to intrude. Hope you're feeling more the thing. I'll leave you now."

"Let me present you first. Miss Verving, this is Captain Allan Jermayne, of the Fourth Dragoon Guards."

The captain reiterated his jerky bow and professed himself to be Cecily's most obedient. Then he said, "Happy to run into you, Brandon. Traveling through Dorset and stopped to see Sir Carolus. He was friends with my father in his school days. He insisted I stay for his party."

He sounded morose, and Lord Brandon asked languidly, "Not enjoyin' the evenin'?"

"Oh, God, no—beg pardon, ma'am. Hell—I don't mean, that, neither," the captain stammered. "More used to battlefields than drawing rooms. Rough tongue. Soldier. Used to foul language. Sorry I swore."

He looked so uncomfortable that Cecily's sympathies were aroused. "I pray that you will not regard it," she said gently. "In certain peoples' company, I often *want* to use foul language."

The captain peered at her, then smiled a shy smile. "Good of you to say so, ma'am. Very kind. But females—I mean, ladies—with fans and gewgaws make me nervous. And the men in fancy dress are worse. Eh? A lot of counter-coxcombs—"

Here his eye fell on Lord Brandon's attire, and he stammered into silence. "It is getting quite cool," Cecily said hastily. "I think we should go in."

Trailed by the captain, Lord Brandon escorted

Cecily back into the drawing room, where members of the orchestra were taking their places. The floor had been cleared for dancing, and chaperons were positioning themselves. Younger ladies were beginning to cast hopeful glances at the cluster of the colonel's Riders, who were still holding forth on the war with the colonies.

"Young muttonheads," Captain Jermayne remarked dispassionately. "Don't look like they know the first thing about war. I wonder what they'd have done in our shoes at Salamanca, Brandon."

"You were at Salamanca together?" Cecily asked, astonished.

The captain nodded. "We were that. I nearly died there. Would have, if Brandon hadn't—"

"Ah, the orchestra has begun," Lord Brandon interrupted. "Will you honor me, Miss Verving?"

Before she knew what he was about, she was in his arms and being whirled away onto the floor in a very fast waltz.

It all happened so quickly that Cecily had no time to protest. And after the first astonished moment, she did not particularly want to protest, for she realized that Lord Brandon was an accomplished dancer.

Almost from the cradle Cecily had loved to dance. Her unconventional parents had encouraged this, and one of her happiest nursery memories was that of waltzing with her laughing young mother while her father accompanied them on the pianoforte.

She had forgotten all about that golden moment, but now as she spun about in Lord Brandon's arms, the memory was rekindled. "Am I going too fast for you, Celia?" he was asking.

Cecily would not admit to a breathlessness caused, no doubt, by the fast pace of the dance.

"To tell you the truth, I do not know why I am

dancing with you," she retorted. "And my name is not Celia."

"It suits you." Cecily felt the surprisingly strong arm around her waist tighten. "You've read what Jonson writes 'To Celia,' haven't you? 'Drink to me only with thine eyes, and I will pledge with mine—'"

"I do not see," Cecily said severely, "that that has anything to do with me. And pray stop singing, Lord Brandon. You are making a cake of yourself."

"—'Or leave a kiss but in the cup, and I'll not look for wine,'" Brandon warbled blithely. "It's only a song, of course. I wasn't suggestin' that you leave kisses lyin' about."

Cecily attempted an icy stare. It was a failure, for the corners of her mouth had begun to twitch suspiciously. "A waste of time," Lord Brandon went on, "leavin' kisses inside cups. There's a much better use for them."

The bold black eyes that rested on her lips were neither sleepy nor lazy, and Cecily found it even more difficult to catch her breath. It was, she thought, high time to end this extremely improper conversation.

Abruptly she changed the subject. "Why did you not want to speak with Captain Jermayne?" she questioned.

"Because I'd rather have the honor of waltzin' with you, naturally."

Not taken in by his guileless smile, Cecily continued, "He said that you were both at Salamanca."

He shuddered. "Not somethin' I like to dwell on, 'pon my honor. It was one of Pershing's maggoty ideas that I join a regiment, and I loathed every minute of it. Now come, Miss Vervant, listen to the music and let it carry you away."

The waltz had slowed, gentled into a softer rhythm. Its dreamy swaying did not ease Cecily's breathlessness, for although Lord Brandon held her the regulation twelve inches away from him, the expression in his eyes drew her closer.

It took some effort to meet that steady black gaze, but she persisted. "So you wish to forget Salamanca?"

"Why wouldn't I want to forget cannons and dirt and smoke? Lord, the smoke. Poor Andrews despaired of keeping my shirts white. He would have given notice if he hadn't been devoted to me. And the food—"

At this moment Sir Carolus, who was dutifully wheeling Lady Breek's eldest daughter about the floor, almost collided with them. Instinctively, Lord Brandon pulled Cecily closer to him, and for a moment she was locked against a body that was whipcord-tough, lean and tight with muscle. And like a hammer blow came knowledge: she had been in this man's arms before.

The waltz ended. Lord Brandon released Cecily and stepped back to bow, and without bothering to dissemble, she searched his face. No. Yes. He *must* be the man who had saved her at the Widow's Rock.

"Miss Vervain, your most obedient. How do you do, ma'am? I am so happy to see you, give you my word."

James Montworthy had shouldered himself between her and Lord Brandon and had taken possession of her hand. Still enmeshed in her tangled thoughts, Cecily barely managed a polite reply.

The conceited young man mistook her preoccupation for missish flutterings. "I didn't see you when you first came in, ma'am," he said soulfully. "Wanted to remind you of our waltz but saw Brandon had stolen a march on me. Didn't think he could bestir himself to waltz, give you m'word."

Cecily gazed after Lord Brandon, who was sauntering across the room. As she watched, he stopped a servant who was passing a tray of small pastries amongst the guests, chose a tidbit, and with elaborate gestures lifted it to his lips.

"A cotillion's starting up, Miss Vervain. I hope you'll honor me," Montworthy was saying.

Cecily allowed Montworthy to lead her to the floor. But while her feet mechanically tapped her way through the cotillion, she kept her eye glued on Lord Brandon.

He had taken a seat next to little Sir Carolus and was seemingly involved in discussing the dinner to come. Cecily noted that Captain Jermayne had come to stand beside them, and that he was looking at Lord Brandon with a thoroughly bewildered expression. Of course the captain would be bewildered, Cecily thought. The captain did not yet realize that Brandon was wearing a mask.

Did his mask cover a smuggler? Lord Brandon was Pershing's eldest son, and in fine old families there was often more ancestral pride than ready cash. Even a duke's son might be tempted by the thought of easy riches.

Cecily realized that James had asked her a question. "You're an incomparable dancer, Miss Vervain," he was saying. "Beg you'll stand up with me again—they'll play a country dance next."

Before Cecily could answer, there was a flurry near the door of the drawing room, and Colonel Howard and his daughter came in.

Even disliking the man as she did, Cecily had to admit that he had presence. Tall and broad-shouldered, erect and of martial carriage, the colonel was more than usually imposing tonight in a steel-gray coat and white breeches of military severity. A medal hung like a star on his white shirt-front, and he wore a ceremonial sword strapped around his waist. One powerful arm was decorated by three strands of gold braid.

He walked among his Riders like a general inspecting his troops, and tripping along in his wake came Delinda. Cecily noted that even while she curtsied to her host, Delinda's blue eyes searched the room for young Montworthy.

Well, there was no accounting for taste, Cecily thought. Aloud she said, "I am afraid I cannot dance the country dance with you, Mr. Montworthy. I do not care for country dances."

"Hoy—don't you?" Montworthy looked momentarily taken aback but recovered himself to ask, "May I hope for a dance later on in the evening, then?"

Just then Colonel Howard bore down upon them. Cecily, who had steeled herself to meet the man's patronizing smile, was grateful when Sir Carolus pattered up to greet his guests. With relief she turned to Delinda, who said in her breathless way, "How do you do, Miss Vervain? Your dress—how very lovely it is. How well you look—I wish I could achieve that effect myself."

Delinda's own round dress had been made of peach satin that did not suit her pale complexion. Her hair had been tortured into ringlets that gave her narrow, anxious face the look of a startled rabbit. She sent Montworthy a wistful look as the orchestra began to play and murmured, "Ah, they are setting up for a country dance. I do love a country dance."

But Montworthy was listening to the colonel and Sir Carolus and did not—or pretended not to—hear. Cecily decided to enter the lists. Smiling at Montworthy, she queried, "I believe that you enjoy country dances, sir?"

James preened himself. He was certain that Cecily was about to change her mind and dance with him. "I do indeed," he said. "Shall we—"

"That is capital," Cecily interrupted heartily. "You and Miss Howard will make a charming pair."

Delinda beamed with pleasure. Montworthy was so astounded that his jaw dropped. "But," he stammered, "Miss Howard has just arrived. Probably fatigued."

"Oh, on the contrary, I assure you that I shall enjoy it above all things—I am not fatigued at all," Delinda protested earnestly.

Cecily felt a sense of satisfaction as she watched the reluctant James lead Delinda toward the floor. Then her attention shifted as she heard Colonel Howard's hectoring voice at her elbow.

"I am sick of hearing about Ghent," he was complaining. "Why should we sit down at a treaty table and try to pacify these colonials? I say we send all our troops across the sea and crush them."

Sir Carolus suggested timidly that this would cost many English lives. The colonel looked scornful. "Patriots feel that death is preferable to dishonor," he declaimed.

His bombast set Cecily's teeth on edge. "My late father was a patriot, sir," she objected, "but he would not agree with you. He often said that England could not afford another war so soon after fighting Bonaparte."

The colonel fairly snorted. "Was your father a soldier?"

"No, but—"

"Either a man is a soldier, or he doesn't know

the first thing about war," the colonel interrupted rudely.

"But I have read that—"

"You have read!" The colonel rolled his eyes, and a sputter of toad-eating laughter ran through the ranks of his Riders. "How can a woman understand military strategy?"

Goaded, Cecily cried, "If you would only see past your own prejudices—"

Raising his voice to drown out hers, Howard lectured, "What I see is that we must take a hard line with these Americans. Their finances are exhausted, their military ready to collapse."

"Now that," commented a drowsy voice, "is a hum."

Lord Brandon had strolled up and was examining the colonel through his quizzing glass. "Where did you hear such brummish stories?" he inquired. "Right now, I'll lay you odds, Boney's gatherin' his forces. He's waitin' for us to escalate the fightin' on the American front. Fightin' a conflict, more's the pity, that we can't win."

The colonel's florid face turned several shades darker. "Are you saying that we may be beaten by *Americans*?" he barked.

"We were before," Lord Brandon pointed out.

He reached a long-fingered hand into his coat pocket, extracted a bejeweled snuffbox, and offered it to the colonel. "My own mixture, Spanish bran, with a touch of Otto of Roses. No? Well, perhaps you prefer Macomber. Don't like it myself, but—"

"Have done with your gabbling," the colonel spluttered. "We were discussing the war. Either contribute to the discussion or be silent."

Lord Brandon looked thoughtful. "We have to face facts. The Americans are fightin' for their

76

homes. If we take the war to America's shores, we'll likely be trounced."

For a moment the colonel stared. Then he found his voice. "That," he thundered, "is treasonous thinking."

"Do you say so?"

The words were drawled softly, but some quality in them caused the hairs on the back of Cecily's neck to quiver erect. Colonel Howard threw out his chest and stiffened his spine to ramrod straightness.

"And what if I do?" he challenged.

"Then I'll call you a brave man." Lord Brandon returned his snuffbox to his pocket, withdrew his musk-scented handkerchief, and touched it delicately to his lips. "You'd be sayin' that half of England was talkin' treason. Landholders want their taxes cut, Howard. Merchants want to sell their goods in peace. One very noble Englishman went so far as to say that we've no right to ask for any concessions of territory from the Americans."

Like Jupiter hurling a thunderbolt, the colonel barked, "And who was *that*? The Duke of *Pershing*?"

"No, the Duke of Wellington," Lord Brandon replied.

The silence that followed this statement was broken by Captain Jermayne, who said, "Struth, that. The Iron Duke's not anxious for another war. Heard him say so myself at Lady Arnstruther's ball."

"So it seems as if you've insulted Wellington," Lord Brandon continued lazily. "If I don't mistake, you as good as called Wellington a traitor." He lifted his quizzing glass and examined the colonel critically. "Not ton to lose your temper, old boy. Brings on the gout, I'm told."

Plump Sir Carolus had been listening to this exchange with mounting anxiety. He now signaled the band to begin a spirited Scottish reel and begged the assembled Riders not to keep the ladies waiting for partners. The Riders, grateful to end this embarrassing discussion, dispersed, and Sir Carolus cast oil on troubled waters.

"My son tells me that you are converting your summerhouse into a military museum, Colonel," he chirruped. "One can think of no one better qualified for such a grand undertaking. Tell me about it, sir, I beg."

"Exit Captain Hackum," Cecily heard Lord Brandon murmur as the little squire led Howard away.

Just then Lady Marcham signaled to Cecily from across the room. She was sitting with several other matrons, and as Cecily came closer, she could hear her grandaunt say, "Used as a gargle, bistort gives great relief to an inflamed throat, Lady Breek. Ah—here is my grandniece come to walk about the room with me. Pray excuse me."

She rose, took Cecily's arm, and practically dragged her away from the other women. "Thank you for rescuing me," she murmured.

"I see that the villagers are not the only ones to ask you for help," Cecily commented.

Lady Marcham made a face. "I shall never understand why some people think their illnesses are fascinating topics of conversation. I collect that I have heard every detail and twitch of Lady Grue's latest affliction. Miss Levellier cannot sleep at night. Major Hamm is afflicted with bunions. All of them profess that they have great faith in Dr. Allardyce—*but*. Tell me, my dear, does anything ail you?"

"Do you have an antidote for Colonel Howard?" Cecily wondered.

"From what I overheard, Trevor has put him in his place." Lady Marcham flicked her jeweled hand as if to rid herself of a nuisance, then added, "Really, it is too bad that the colonel decided to retire here in Dorset. The Duchess of Fullerhill confided in me that even in his regiment he was misliked because of his ungovernable temper and bullying tongue."

"No wonder his daughter seemed afraid of her own shadow," Cecily said, and Lady Marcham nodded.

"Poor Delinda. Her late mother was apparently a spiritless person, and like mother, like daughter. How did you manage to get James to stand up with her?"

Out of the corner of her eye Cecily noted that James was still hopping up and down with Delinda and that he wore a very disgusted expression. "The question is why she wants to stand up with *him*," Cecily said.

"James is a handsome figure of a man, a Corinthian," Lady Marcham commented placidly. "He dances adequately also, though Trevor is better, is he not?"

"Lord Brandon is full of surprises." Cecily gave her aunt a thoughtful look. "I did not know that he had been at Salamanca until Captain Jermayne told me so. Apparently they served on the Peninsula together."

Lady Marcham looked vaguely interested. "Oh, is one of his comrades from his regiment here? I must invite this Captain Jermayne to call. As to Trevor, still waters, you know, run deep, and sometimes they run dangerously swift."

Was Aunt Emerald *warning* her? Instinctively Cecily glanced toward Lord Brandon. He was almost recumbent in his chair and had his eyes closed. The brief energy with which he had faced

Colonel Howard had seemingly evaporated. There could be no possible danger associated with this man. He looked incapable of doing anything but falling asleep.

But then he stirred in his chair, and Cecily saw his lion's ring catch the light. There was no question that still waters ran deep. The question was, where did they lead?

Cecily stood by her bedroom window and listened to the distant waves beating against the Widow's Rock. It was three in the morning, and Marcham Place had been asleep for hours. Even Archimedes lay sprawled belly-up at the foot of the bed, but she herself felt restive and troubled and as far away from sleep as she was from the full moon behind the scudding clouds.

"Who are you, Lord Brandon?" she asked of the night.

The world knew him as the eldest son of the Ice Duke. He was well known to be a great dandy. Many considered him a useless fop. Yet the fop had knowledge of national policy and public opinion, and the dandy's tongue had a cutting edge. He could ride as few men could, and apparently he could fight as well, for Captain Jermayne's greeting had been to a respected comrade-in-arms. And there was another facet to the man as well. When they had danced, when they had stood together on the balcony—

There was a noise below her window, and Cecily saw a figure walking briskly toward the herb garden. When he turned his head and looked back at the house, moonlight silvered Lord Brandon's face. For a second he stood still, as though listening for some sound. Then he began to stride through the rose garden and in a few moments had disappeared down the path toward the woods.

A low grumbling purr erupted at Cecily's feet, and a shaggy head rubbed against her knee. Archimedes had woken up. She picked up the old cat, noting that he was much heavier than when they had arrived at Marcham Place. Mary, convinced in her superstitious soul that Archimedes was in league with witches, had enlisted Mrs. Horris's aid and was propitiating him with offerings of food.

"Tell me, Archimedes," Cecily said aloud, "why should Lord Brandon be walking about in the Haunted Woods at night?" The cat wriggled and growled. "I know you like him, but there is something decidedly smoky about him. I am persuaded that he is a smuggler after all. But wait—here comes another man."

The newcomer was tall and lean. He did not walk with Lord Brandon's lithe stride but moved in a surreptitious manner. Was this yet another smuggler—Lord Brandon's confederate, perhaps? Cecily leaned over the windowsill to look, but as the second shadow appeared on the garden path, the moon slid behind a cloud bank. When it reappeared, the second man had disappeared.

"I think I will watch and see who comes out," Cecily mused. She drew a chair to the window, positioned the cat on her lap, and settled down to wait.

It was nearly an hour before Lord Brandon reappeared and made his way back to the house. This time he looked up as he passed Cecily's window, and she instinctively drew back. It was almost, Cecily thought, as though he were looking for her.

What Lord Brandon did was no concern of hers, but it did concern her Aunt Emerald. Cecily frowned into the darkness. If he was breaking the law, he was putting Lady Marcham in a difficult position. Not only was he her godson and thus dear to her, but Lady Marcham herself could be accused of being his accomplice. "I cannot let that happen," Cecily said thoughtfully, "but I cannot accuse him without proof. I must find out more."

She slept fitfully that night, and dawn found her awake and dressed. When Mary appeared with the morning tea, Cecily was already settling her pelisse around her shoulders.

The abigail looked scandalized. "Holy saints above, ma'am," she exclaimed, "where are you off to at such an hour?"

"I thought I would go for a walk in the woods," Cecily began, but Mary immediately crossed herself and invoked the names of all the saints.

"Save us, and aren't the Haunted Woods a horrible place?" she keened. "It's said that the little people themselves put a word on the late master's horse. They're out there still, the elves and piskies and hobgoblins that come out and dance through the night."

"But it is broad daylight," Cecily pointed out.

"Day or night makes no matter," Mary retorted. "Sure, and those woods are not safe. Lady Marcham agrees, too, for didn't she have the groundkeeper's cottage torn down after my lord met his death? There is no more hunting or riding done there anymore."

Her warnings followed Cecily out of the room and down the stairs, and it was a relief to step into the cloudy day and walk down the garden path toward the woods. No one was about at this early hour, but as Cecily was about to step into the trees that bordered the woods, a familiar voice spoke behind her.

"Highly unwise, 'pon my honor," Lord Brandon drawled. "Wouldn't do that if I were you."

At the sound of his voice Cecily's heart seemed

to stop. Then it commenced pounding. It took an effort to turn to face him and ask, "Why?"

"Shoes, ma'am," was the prompt reply.

"Shoes," she repeated blankly.

He tapped the ground with the tip of his walking stick. "It rained pitchforks and shovels toward dawn, Miss Verving. See the mud? Walk into the woods, and your shoes will be ruined."

"And that will never do," she said sarcastically.

She regarded Brandon. His eyes were again hooded, and from his polished boots to his buff coat with enormous brass buttons, he was every inch the dandy.

He raised a languid hand to pat back a yawn before saying, "I went walking there once after coming to Dorset, and I can tell you that I ruined a perfectly good pair of boots."

"And did you not ruin your shoes last night when you walked in the woods?" she challenged.

The look that met hers was as bland as a baby's— and about as blank. "Eh?" his lordship asked. "What's that? *Me* walk at night?" 'Pon my honor, Miss Verving, I did no such thing."

"But I saw—"

"You didn't see *me*," his lordship insisted. "I thought I told you once that the night air is ruinous to a man's complexion. Besides, I was sound asleep all night."

"Were you indeed?" Cecily murmured.

She turned her back on him and began to walk into the line of trees. "So you're determined." Lord Brandon sighed. "In that case there's nothin' for it—I'll come with you. I can't shirk my responsibilities as a gentleman."

"You have no responsibility to me," Cecily retorted. "I am perfectly capable of managing my own affairs. Besides, I could not bear to have you torture your shoes."

He took her sarcasm at face value. "Andrews will be in a takin', but what can I do? I can't fight shy and abandon a female in unfamiliar terrain. See, there's the path that leads into the woods. Muddy, as I said."

The path was small and, as Lord Brandon had warned, very wet. Cecily sank up to her ankles almost at once. "Where does this path lead?" she asked as she attempted to extricate herself from the mud.

"To the old groundkeeper's cottage, I expect." Lord Brandon sounded glum. "Lady M. had it dismantled after Marcham died. He used to be a keen huntsman, Marcham, and I suppose she couldn't bear to be reminded of him. Do you know their story, Miss Verving?"

Plodding determinedly through the mud, Cecily shook her head.

"Marcham was one of the wealthiest peers of his generation," Lord Brandon began. "His family wanted him to marry the plump-pursed Countess of Lesserford. It'd been arranged by both the families since the principals were in leadin' strings. But then Marcham saw Lady Emerald and fell in love with her—and she with him. Of course there was trouble."

In spite of the fact that she was sure that Lord Brandon was talking to distract her, Cecily was interested. "Trouble from Lord Marcham's family, you mean?"

"And from hers, too. Lady M. was the second daughter of Lord and Lady Veere, and the beauty of the season. She had earls and nabobs danglin' after her. Offers fell like ripe plums at her feet. Even the pater—this was before he met my mother—fell head over heels in love with her. But she chose Marcham and remained true to him till he died."

Lord Brandon paused. "Faithful to him *after* he died, actually. Lady M. was still beautiful enough and rich enough to have married many times over, but she has never looked at another man."

His voice seemed to echo among the gnarled trees and sigh away into the woods. His words awoke a memory. "I once asked Father why he did not marry again," Cecily heard herself say.

"And what was his answer?"

"That for certain people love comes only once. He said that he did not know whether that was a blessing or a curse, but that was the way it was."

Lord Brandon said nothing. He simply walked beside her, listening, and after a pause Cecily continued, "My father was lonely after Mother died. If he had married a good, kind woman, she would have brightened his days."

Brandon was watching the shadows grow in her eyes. "And you," he could not help but say, "were you lonely, too?"

"I do not know," Cecily replied truthfully. "I had my father, you see. But sometimes when I saw him look at Mother's portrait and smile, it made me sad. I suppose it was because I could not share his memories."

"You need not envy him. You will have memories of your own."

His voice had changed. It was softer, almost as soft as the dark shadows thrown by the surrounding trees. It was cool under those trees, cool and rich with the scents of new-turned earth and moss and greenery. A golden butterfly danced ahead of them, like a promise.

With her eyes on those shimmering wings, Cecily

spoke almost to herself. "I wonder what kind of memories they will be."

"Happy ones," he told her. "You have my promise on that, Celia."

His name for her brought back reality. Cecily did not know what she had been thinking about.

Since her father's death, she had not talked about him or about her feelings with anyone, and yet here she was confiding her innermost thoughts to the outrageous Lord Brandon. She felt embarrassed and annoyed at herself and at him. Perhaps he was secretly laughing at her.

But there was no laughter in his face or voice as he said, "Your father understood that though marriage in our class is usually a matter of convenience, once in a while the equation changes. No one asks for love to come, perhaps would rather not have it come, but if it does, it changes everything."

An almost dreamlike quality held Cecily enthralled. She found herself holding her breath as Lord Brandon continued. "I think I understand how your father felt. When a man has seen the sun, neither the moon nor all the stars will satisfy him."

When she looked at him like that, with her gray eyes softened to silver and her lips curving softly, Brandon tore his wandering mind back from ruinous thoughts and clasped his hands behind his back. Fool, he warned himself, take care or you will ruin everything.

Smuggler, fop, or knave, it did not matter—the man beside her was unlike any man she had ever known. But before that thought could take hold in Cecily's mind, Brandon was speaking again.

"Here the path ends," he said in his old die-away drawl. "Do you see the thicket that has grown around what's left of the groundkeeper's cottage?'Pon my honor, Lady M. should do something about this eyesore."

With a feeling of anticlimax, Cecily looked at the tumbledown cottage. As Lord Brandon had pointed out, the place was a hideous ruin. Not even the most desperate criminals could have used it as a meeting place. She looked beyond the mess to a thick growth of alder trees and then at the muddy ground. She could see no sign of footprints. Wherever the duke's son had gone the night before, it was not here.

"Satisfied, Miss Verving?" Lord Brandon asked.

Suddenly she wondered why she had even bothered to investigate the woods. She did not care a rush whether Lord Brandon was a smuggler or not, and Lady Marcham could obviously take care of herself.

"Thank you, I am quite satisfied," Cecily said stiffly.

But as she turned to retrace her steps, her foot caught a root submerged in the mud. She stumbled and would have fallen if Lord Brandon had not caught her in his arms.

For a moment black eyes met wide gray ones, and the world seemed to go very still. The insect drone around them hushed, and even the wind held its peace. Cecily tried for a bracing breath and drew in not musk but a strong, clean, virile scent that was Lord Brandon's own. His arms held her so easily, and against her softness she felt the steady beat of his heart.

For a moment his eyes held hers, and then it was as though a shutter had come crashing down. Lord Brandon blinked, smiled, and drawled, "Warned you about that mud, didn't I? Well, no damage done, ma'am, but we should lose no time gettin' back to the house. Unless I miss my guess, it's past breakfast time."

Chapter Six

Lord Brandon watched Cecily across the breakfast table and thought for perhaps the hundredth time that he had not expected his work in Dorset to be so difficult.

He had expected danger and unforeseen problems, and though he had not calculated on Colonel Howard's interference, he was dealing with the man in his own way. Cecily, however . . .

As if aware that he was thinking of her, she looked up, and her gray eyes were dark with suspicion. Brandon blamed himself for that. The incident at the Widow's Rock had been unfortunate, but last night on Sir Carolus's balcony had been sheer lunacy. And he had compounded that folly this morning. If he had not come to his senses at the last moment . . .

"More tea, dear boy?"

With difficulty Brandon pulled himself back to reality and drawled, "Indeed. Where would we be without tea? A most excellent potation in the mornin', 'pon my honor. But you are not eatin',

Miss Verving. I hope you have not caught a chill in the woods."

Brandon had devoured a dish of kidneys and ham, lamb chops done to a turn, and eggs served up as only the skillful Mrs. Horris could cook them. Watching him, Cecily could not help wondering if she were not mistaken about the previous night's events. Lord Brandon seemed incapable of anything more energetic than lifting his fork.

But then she looked into her grandaunt's smiling eyes and felt her worries return. Colonel Howard was a tyrant and a bully, and he and his Riders would eventually run the brethren of the coast to earth. If the Duke of Pershing's son was one of the smugglers, his rank would not save him. And those who gave him comfort would not be spared.

So vivid were these thoughts that when Grigg entered the room to announce a visitor, Cecily started. She envisioned Colonel Howard striding into the room to arrest Lord Brandon and accuse Lady Marcham of being his accomplice, but their visitor was only Delinda.

As usual, Delinda's costume was expensive and ugly. Though her bonnet of lavender chip straw tied with ribbons might have come from the best milliner in Bond Street, it had a distinctly dowdy look, and her walking dress of sprigged muslin made her appear even taller and bonier than she was.

"Good morning, dear Lady Marcham," Delinda breathed. "Good day, Miss Vervain, Lord Brandon. I hope I am not intruding. It is, after all, so early—"

"It is never too early," Lord Brandon interrupted. He rose and bowed with sleepy gallantry as he added, "It's always a pleasure to see you, ma'am."

The flustered Delinda curtsied and dropped her

reticule. "Oh—forgive me," she stammered as his lordship retrieved it. "Papa says that I am fumble-fingered and as clumsy as a plow horse."

That was exactly what a clod like the colonel would say, Brandon thought. He returned the reticule with another bow saying, "He does you an injustice, ma'am."

"I collect that he has reason," Delinda said mournfully. "I am so clumsy—I drop things everywhere. I fear that I am sadly wanting."

"Another injustice. I find you most delightful in all things, ma'am."

Cecily felt a rush of warmth for Lord Brandon. He was probably guilty of many things, but he was kind, too. She decided that, smuggler or not, she did not want the colonel to trap him.

"Fathers don't often see that their daughters are diamonds of the first water," Lord Brandon was saying. "Were it not time for me to take my mornin' perambulations, I'd beg to be permitted to share your company, Miss Howard. The loss is mine, 'pon my honor."

Excusing himself he sauntered off, and Delinda said resolutely, "Lady Marcham, there is a reason I have come—"

She broke off, looking confused. Lady Marcham said kindly, "You are nervous, child. I have an infusion of sage that will make you feel more the thing. If you come to my stillroom, I will give you some to take home with you."

Delinda murmured her thanks but glanced pointedly at Cecily. "If you will excuse me also," Cecily was beginning, but Lady Marcham shook her head.

"No, you must come with us. Delinda will be glad of your company."

Delinda looked anything but pleased, but she did not dispute Lady Marcham. "It will take a moment to prepare the tonic," Lady Marcham said as she led the way to the stillroom. "I will also infuse for you some tea of broom flowers and dandelion root and juniper berries. It is my secret recipe for a digestive tonic."

While Cecily assisted her grandaunt, Delinda walked about the stillroom. She paused before the book of herbs that Lady Marcham's grandmother had illustrated, and exclaimed, "What wonderful drawings. May I look at them?"

She began to leaf through the pages and became so absorbed that she did not at first hear Cecily come up behind her. Then she started, blushed a fiery red, and slammed the book shut.

"I beg you will not spy on me," she cried.

Cecily was astonished. "I did not mean to spy on you," she protested. "Whatever is the matter with you?"

To her surprise two tears appeared at the corners of Delinda's eyes. "Forgive me," she sobbed. "I have not been truthful. I did not come for a remedy for headache." She gulped hard and whispered, "Lady Marcham, could you—would you make me a ... a love potion?"

There was a moment of silence before Lady Marcham laughed. "You are funning me."

"There must be a recipe for a love potion in your books," Delinda pleaded. "There is a page entitled, 'The ancient uses of verbenum in a love philter.'"

"Oh, that. The ancient Romans had some such notion, but that is because verbena has such a pleasant fragrance. La, child, people in the Dark Ages believed in a great deal of humgudgeon, including witchcraft. I *hope* you do not think I am a witch, Delinda?"

"Of course not. I beg your pardon—I did not mean to be insulting." Distressed, Delinda clasped and unclasped her hands. "I have given you a disgust of me, Lady Marcham, and I am sorry, but I—I am beside the bridge. *He* never notices me." Two new tears welled over her eyes and slid down her cheeks. "He loves another."

"If you mean that James Montworthy loves me," Cecily said frankly, "I tell you to your head that he does not. He only throws sheep's eyes at me because he is bored in Dorset."

Delinda looked shocked at such plain speaking, but her emotions caused her to quaver, "Then you do not return his regard, Miss Vervain?"

"I have told you, there is no regard. And even if there were, I could not return it. So you need not want to scratch my eyes out after all."

She smiled cheerfully at Delinda, who managed a faint answering smile. "I am sorry," she murmured. "I did not know. But—but Lady Marcham, is there really *no* potion that will make Mr. Montworthy notice me?"

"Not unless I could dose him with common sense," Lady Marcham replied somewhat impatiently. "I have known him since he was in leading strings, and though he is not a bad boy, he was badly spoiled by his late mother. And Sir Carolus has not made his son come up to the mark, even though James has lost so much money in the gaming hells." She paused. "I agree with you that he looks well in his gold braid, but I do not think he in the least resembles the young Lochinvar."

Delinda, who had been bristling at criticisms of her beloved James, stared at Lady Marcham. "Oh," she gasped, "how could you know that I—"

"Mind you," Lady Marcham interrupted, "I have always considered that the young Lochinvar was a nincompoop. To snatch a bride from her wedding festivities and throw her over the saddle for a gallop across the border—*well*! This kind of behavior may serve for totty-headed gentlemen who consider themselves Corinthians, but what the bride's mother said to her assembled guests I cannot begin to guess. Truly intolerable, my dear. And it is also intolerable that your father's sapskull Riders were racketing around my woods last night."

Delinda's eyes widened at this rapid change of subject. "They must have been patrolling the sea road. Papa believes that the smugglers have been landing at Robin's Cove," she explained feebly.

"All they will find is night mist and owls. It will serve them right if they catch the grippe." Lady Marcham broke off and patted Delinda's cheek apologetically. "I did not mean to rail at you, dear child. Take this thyme mixture and the broom tea, and you will feel less down pin."

With this she left the stillroom. Delinda stood clutching the two phials to her chest and looked longingly at the book of herbs. "Have you looked all through the book, Miss Vervain?" she asked.

"Please, call me Cecily. And, yes, I have read the book."

Delinda looked so sorrowful that Cecily's heart ached for her. "My late father used to quote Hecaton of Rhodes," she said gently. "I remember him saying, 'I will reveal to you a love potion—' "

Delinda clasped her hands together. "Yes, yes?"

" '—without medicine, without herbs, without any witch's magic. If you want to be loved, then love.' You do not need a love potion, Delinda, really."

Delinda drooped even more. "I wish I knew what to do. You are beautiful and sure of yourself and would never be at a loss like me. Cecily, Mr. Montworthy does not even know I exist. But I—oh, look!"

Through the window Cecily could see a familiar figure on a bay gelding galloping up to the house. He was followed by Captain Jermayne.

Delinda had begun to tremble. "*He* is here," she faltered, adding gloomily, "He has come to see you, of course."

"But he will not see me," Cecily promised. "I must go into the village to take the widow Amber some ointment. Go and meet James and help Aunt Emerald entertain the gentlemen, Delinda. I will slip out of the back way."

Cecily had originally intended to take the trap to Wickart-on-Sea, but once outside, she saw that the day had turned sunny. There was a westerly breeze that made it quite warm and pleasant, and besides, she felt in need of exercise. Setting her grandaunt's basket of medicines over her arm, Cecily set out to walk briskly along the sea road.

She did not know why she felt so lighthearted until it occurred to her that this was the first time she had gone out alone since arriving at Marcham Place. Always before this she had been in the company of her aunt or attended by a servant, and that morning there had been Lord Brandon. Cecily's dark brows puckered as she recalled his lordship's sudden appearance.

What was he doing in those woods? she wondered.

She had seen nothing except a torn-down groundkeeper's hut and a path that ended in a thicket of trees. That and mud, and hidden roots that had caused her to stumble into Lord Brandon's arms—

Hastily turning her mind from discomfiting memories, Cecily put thoughts of Lord Brandon aside and concentrated instead on Delinda's problem. And she did have a problem. There was no way the sap-skulled Corinthian was going to notice Delinda unless she had some help.

Cecily's thoughts were interrupted by a gull that swooped down close to her. She stopped walking to admire the snow-white bird and then realized that at this point the sea road almost melted into the sand. It was low tide, and a long sweep of sandbar lay exposed by the retreating water. When she followed the thick line of gold with her eyes, Cecily saw that it stretched past the Widow's Rock and actually led to Wickart-on-Sea.

The smell of salt was raw and intoxicating. As Cecily watched sunlight dance invitingly on the blue waters and on the distant spire of the village church, another memory surfaced. When she was five or six, she had once accompanied her parents to the seaside. She had taken off her shoes and stockings and gone wading in the cool water, where she had splashed and tried to catch fish. She had collected shells and even found an indignant hermit crab.

The memory of that day—her parents' happy faces, the sun, and the sound of gulls swooping overhead—all brought an ache of homesickness for times that could never return. Cecily looked about her and saw that no one was nearby. What harm would it do if she walked to the village across the sandbar?

She sat down on a convenient rock and rolled off her stockings. Then she put them and her shoes into her basket, hitched up her skirts, and ventured out onto the sand. The silky sand was cool between her toes, and when she reached the water, the feel of it was wonderfully cool, also.

Barefoot, with her skirts looped high over her ankles, Cecily began to walk over the damp sandbar. Memories of her parents seemed very close, and as she strolled along, she smiled to recall them as they had been—not sickly or old or poor but young and full of life and joy. How beautiful they had been, she thought, and inconsequentially remembered Lord Brandon's words. "When a man has seen the sun, neither the moon nor all the stars will satisfy him."

"Go away," Cecily told Lord Brandon. "Stop bothering me."

She took a step forward and sank up to her ankle in water. Surprised, Cecily looked about her. She had been so lost in thoughts of her childhood that she had not fully realized she had walked almost into the shadow of the Widow's Rock.

"Oh, good heavens!" she exclaimed.

While she was walking, the tide had started to come in, and the sandbar on which she was standing was surrounded by water. Cecily tested the depth of that water and sank up to her knees.

"What a fool I am," Cecily exclaimed.

As she attempted to retreat, the sand under her feet seemed to be yanked away. There was a riptide there—a very strong one. For the first time, Cecily was worried.

Ahead of her hulked the dark fist of the Widow's Rock. Behind her stretched miles of sparkling blue sea. There was no one about, no one who could help. Cecily backtracked away from the riptide thinking, I will have to go another way.

But what other way was there? As the thought touched her mind, she heard a halloo across the water and saw a man standing on the shore. Even though the light was at his back, Cecily recognized Lord Brandon. Not bothering to wonder where he had come from, she waved frantically at him.

"You look as if you are in trouble," Lord Brandon called.

She nodded vigorously. "Can you get someone to come and help me? A fisherman with a boat, perhaps?"

"No time for that. The tide comes in swiftly hereabouts. Stay where you are."

He didn't mean to come after her himself? But apparently that was just what he was about to do. As Cecily watched, Lord Brandon removed his tasseled boots, took off his jacket and waistcoat, peeled off his silk stockings, and rolled up his breeches to the knee. Then, to Cecily's shocked surprise, he also removed his shirt.

"What are you doing?" she asked nervously.

"Only a fool goes swimmin' fully dressed." As calmly as though he were going on a stroll around the garden, Lord Brandon waded into the water.

"How did you get all the way out there?" he wanted to know.

"I thought that I could walk to the village across the sandbar. I did not pay any attention to the tide. Oh—be careful," Cecily cried, as Brandon sank up to his chest in water. "There is a strong riptide here."

"You forget that I know these waters very well." But while Brandon was mouthing these words, he was thinking that he had never seen Cecily look so charming. With her hair tousled by the wind, her skirt hem tucked up and wet, her feet bare, she looked irresistible.

"Cully and I used to swim and crab around here," he reminded her. "Don't worry. I'm a strong swimmer."

"So am I," she said, "but I do not trust that riptide. Besides, these herbs would be lost if I tried to swim for it."

"Neither you nor the herbs will come to harm," he said. He had reached the sandbar, and she noted that he was dripping wet. His breeches clung to his lean hips and horseman's thighs, and water droplets glinted on his bare chest. The effect was disquieting in the extreme.

"I am sorry," Cecily said stiffly, "that I have behaved in such an idiotic way. I fear that I have inconvenienced you horribly, sir."

"Don't regard it, Miss Verving. It's not every day that I'm allowed to rescue a maiden in distress."

He took a step closer to her. Instinctively she retreated. "What are you going to do?"

"To carry you to the shore," Lord Brandon announced. As he spoke, he lifted Cecily into his arms and held her quite effortlessly. "Watch out for the basket, Celia."

She knew that she should tell him not to address her so familiarly, but that was not so easy when she was in his arms, with her own arm wrapped around his neck. At such close quarters Cecily was conscious of the fact that Lord Brandon's hair was deep gold, almost the color of honey, and that it curled at the nape of his neck. She noted the small white scar behind his ear and the curve of his lips. The warmth of his body reached her even through their wet clothing.

Cecily felt dizzy, as though her brain was not getting enough oxygen. In order to say something—anything to break the charged silence between them—she said, "You are right about the tide. It is rising very quickly."

"In Dorset many things happen quickly."

Was it her imagination that his arms tightened about her? Cecily did not care for the leap of her pulse. "I am very grateful to you, sir," she said formally.

To listen to her, she was as cool as an ice maiden. Yet her gray eyes were full of uncertainty, and her mouth was soft and definitely kissable. Brandon had to fight with himself to concentrate on what she was saying—something about the Widow's Rock.

"It is fortunate for me that you arrived when you did," Cecily was saying. "I did not know you came as far as the Widow's Rock on your morning walk."

"I do sometimes."

Something in the ease with which he replied told her that he was lying. "Did you have a pleasant visit with Captain Jermayne?" she wondered.

"Jermayne?" Lord Brandon drawled. "Was he at Marcham Place? I'm sorry I missed him, 'pon my honor."

Which was another lie. Cecily was sure that Lord Brandon had seen the captain ride up. Rather than face a man who could penetrate his disguise, the duke's son had slipped away. "Captain Jermayne knows you well, does he not?" she queried. "After all, you were comrades-in-arms."

"I wish, Miss Verving, that you will stop referrin' to my military career. It was a lamentable business, 'pon my honor."

"Then we will talk of something else. We are passing the Widow's Rock, where the mysterious rider rescued the mail coach. Do you believe that he was a smuggler, Lord Brandon?"

"Not bein' in the confidence of the brethren of the coast," he pointed out, "I don't know the answer to that."

"What a gallant man he was—and he wore a ring like yours, too. I wonder—"

Cecily's words broke off in a little shriek as Lord Brandon missed his footing and nearly fell. Cecily clasped him about the neck. Her basket flew one way, and she almost flew the other. She gave an involuntary cry as the water reached out for her.

"It's all right, I have you."

Brandon could feel her tremble in his arms. There was a light in her eyes, and her mouth was a rosy flower. A fierce need to kiss that mouth rose in him.

His arms were around her, holding her tightly clasped against the hard wall of his chest. Cecily registered this fact a moment before she saw the look in his eyes. The next moment, his lips had found hers.

His mouth was cool and sure. He tasted of salt and warmth and of some ineffably wonderful ingredient that caught at her heart. The constant mutter of the ocean, the cries of the gull, even the warmth of the sun died into a stillness broken only by the pounding of her own pulse.

He had not meant to do this, had not meant to kiss her, *must* not kiss her—warning voices were shouting in Brandon's brain advising him of his folly. He ignored them. Nothing seemed to matter to him, nothing would ever matter again except the woman in his arms. He breathed in her subtle flower scent, tasted the trembling sweetness of her lips. He would never, could not ever, let her go.

A sea gull swooped low, screamed almost in their ears. Cecily did not even hear it. There seemed to be a wildness in her blood, and she was as breathless as though she had been whirled about in a dance. She felt dizzy and unbalanced, but at the same time she had never before felt so completely alive.

But though she did not heed the sea gull, Brandon did. Of a sudden the dazzlement in his mind cleared, and he felt the pull of the undertow beneath his feet. Underlying the surge of his emotions, the chill voice of his sanity was reasserting itself. What he was here in Dorset to do was too important to set aside.

Though to do so was unspeakably hard, Brandon forced himself to stop kissing Cecily and asked, "The ground is treacherous hereabouts. Are you all right, Celia?"

His drawl was forced. His voice sounded raw with the effort it took to control it, but she did not hear that note, for she was busy fighting her own battles.

"That is not my name," she tried to say sternly, but to her annoyance, there was a quiver in her voice. "Please put me down so that I can retrieve my basket."

The slight tremor in her voice made Brandon want to draw her close to him again. Instead he said, "A few more steps and we'll be on terra firma. Ah, here we are."

He set her down on the damp sand, then turned away to catch her basket out of a wave. "Somewhat wet but none the worse for wear," he commented. "If I know Lady M.'s potations, they'll be better for a dash of salt water."

Their hands touched as Cecily took the basket from him. Even this fleeting, accidental contact made her feel as though a lightning bolt had stroked her skin. Hastily she took several steps backward away from him.

"You had better put on your shoes and your stockin's," Lord Brandon suggested. "It's a long walk to the village."

In silence she wrung out her dripping skirts and put on her hose and shoes. Then he said, "Let me carry the basket to the village for you."

When she turned, she saw him fully dressed. Except for his wet breeches, he looked as he always did. "It is not necessary," she replied.

"It is to me. You see, Miss Verving, I confess that I behaved out of character today." Lord Brandon pulled his snuffbox from his pocket and snapped it open. "I so seldom am called on to perform heroic acts that I was carried away by the romance of the moment. I assure you I forgot myself entirely. My, er, actions were not worthy of a gentleman. I beg you to forgive me."

Cecily raised her chin and watched him inhaling snuff. He must think very little of her intelligence, she thought wrathfully, if he felt he could fob her off with Bambury tales.

Lord Brandon did not fool her for a moment. He had kissed her not because he was carried away by the moment but because he wanted to end an uncomfortable discussion.

In his own way Lord Brandon was as smug as James Montworthy. He was certainly as odious.

"Of course," she told him, coldly. "No apology is necessary."

"You are too good. But in penance, allow me to carry your basket to the village, Miss Verving." He looked down at his sopping breeches. "From Wickart-on-Sea I can send a message to Andrews so that he can bring me some dry clothes. He will probably swoon when he sees the condition I'm in, but anythin' is preferable to walkin' into Marcham Place lookin' like this. My reputation would be ruined."

In silence Cecily handed him her basket. Let his deceitful lordship accompany her to the village or go to Jericho as he willed, she thought; it was all one to her.

Chapter Seven

Turning her back on Lord Brandon, Cecily began to trudge toward the village. She was determined not to turn around and see whether he was following, but the silence stretched and stretched. Perhaps he had changed his mind and was not coming after all, she thought.

Cecily glanced over her shoulder and looked straight into his dark eyes. "Ah," he drawled, "the fair damsel relents and forgives me."

"There is nothing to forgive, Lord Brandon."

Brandon smiled at her icy tone. "Kind of you to say so, 'pon my honor. Whether Andrews will ever forgive me for going wadin' in my clothes is another matter. If they saw me now, my friends would give me the cut direct."

"I wonder that you do not return to London," Cecily snapped.

"It's too hot at this time of year. Stiflin'. The stench would be excruciatin' for someone with delicate sensibilities." Lord Brandon waved a languid hand. "Besides, I am very fond of Lady M."

It was almost on the tip of Cecily's tongue to ask

him why, if he was so fond of his godmother, he was running the risk of embroiling her in his schemes. With difficulty she reminded herself that she had no proof of his involvement with the smugglers.

Lord Brandon continued, "I used to come to Dorset every summer until I was twelve. My brothers, all several years younger than I was, stayed home in Pershing, but I begged to come here."

Cecily remained dampeningly silent. This did not deter Brandon, who drawled on, "My mother, the duchess, was a busy woman. She had her hands full with arrangin' and attendin' balls and assemblies and musical evenin's. She had the younger boys and our sister to deal with, too—Elizabeth's come-out is still the talk of the ton—so she was glad to pack me off to Lady M."

In spite of herself, interest stirred. Cecily rationalized that if she could get Lord Brandon talking about himself, he might make some incriminating slip.

"Did your father also wish to send you to Dorset?" she asked.

"Pershing was rarely home. He was a soldier while I was growin' up, always away on some military campaign. Then Mother died, and he turned to politics. But whenever he was in residence at Pershing, we toed the mark."

While he spoke, Brandon saw his father clearly. With his dark, flashing eyes, decisive voice, and air of command, he had won battles on the field and in parliament by sheer force of personality. Men were anxious to stay in his good graces, and it was rumored that even Wellington did not care to cross the Ice Duke.

"When he gave a command, we obeyed—that was about the sum of our relationship with Pershing." Cecily noted the dry note in Lord Brandon's voice as he added, "His mission was to make men of all of us. No easy task."

Not for poor, shiftless Leonard, who rebelled against authority and spent years in useless profligacy before marrying and raising a quiverful of brats as unruly as himself. Not easy for bookish Thomas, either, though Thomas was almost as stubborn as his sire and had become a cleric in spite of Pershing. Easier for Clarence, who had been their mother's favorite—a sweet-tempered if emptyheaded lad who embraced a military career as though born to it. And as for himself . . .

For a moment Brandon contemplated his reasons for being in Dorset and the effect that his recent actions would have on the duke.

"Our father was a hard man to bridge at the best of times," he continued at last. "Dorset was my favorite place because here I could run tame in and out of Lady M.'s house. In a way it was my only real childhood."

Though Lord Brandon's tone was casual, Cecily felt a quiver of sympathy. A scene from her own childhood had touched her mind, and she recalled an impromptu picnic. Her mother had spread a white cloth and put out bread, cheese, and honey and apples, and her father had read aloud from Tacitus while Cecily made daisy chains for them all. Later, when Father was old and ill and they were always in need of money, it had helped to remember the scent of daisies and the taste of apples and the sounds of happiness.

"Not everyone has a magical childhood." Surprised out of her thoughts, Cecily looked up and saw Lord Brandon watching her. "You didn't tell me if you lived in the country. Did you?"

"In Sussex. My father was a scholar who loved his books and nature." Cecily's eyes sparkled as she added, "He had a small living, and my mother had her marriage portion. It was not very much, but it seemed more than enough to me. We had a comfortable little home and all sorts of animals. We had a tame squirrel, and a raven, and a poor old badger that we rescued from a trap."

"And cats?"

"Archimedes was a kitten when my mother died."

Brandon saw her smile fade and memories darken her eyes and thought that she had the most expressive eyes he had ever seen. He was used to people who had secrets to conceal or games of their own to play, but by looking into Cecily Vervain's eyes, he felt he could look directly into her heart.

And just now, her heart was troubled. He could guess the reason and wished that he could say something to reassure her. But, he reasoned, the truth would probably alarm her even more than her suspicions.

"That cat of yours has terrorized the whole household," he said aloud. "Even Andrews, who has never been afraid of anythin', turns pale when Archimedes lifts his lip and hisses."

"I have *tried* to make him behave, but he will not. Archimedes does not like too many people," Cecily admitted. "He did not care for anyone at the Netherbys', certainly. The Netherbys were my employers before I—before I came to Marcham Place."

Brandon noted the slight hesitation in her voice. Without seeming too curious, he drawled, "Perhaps there was a reason for him not likin' these Netherbys?"

"Indeed, there was. Master Giles Netherby, especially, was a care-for-nobody who kicked poor Archimedes whenever he could." Cecily's darkling look spoke volumes, and Brandon found himself wishing that he had the care-for-nobody close to his fist. "The curious thing," Cecily continued, "is that Archimedes likes both you and Aunt Emerald. It is most strange."

"He's attracted to my sterlin' character. He knows that I am to be trusted and relied on."

She looked up quickly at this, and the look in his eyes made her catch her breath. For an instant it was as though a very different man was looking out from Lord Brandon's black eyes. Then the fop came back.

"Of course," Lord Brandon drawled, "cat hairs are somethin' else again. Andrews almost went wild the last time your animal brushed up against my coat. Took him an hour to get it clean."

Cecily was disgusted with herself. Once again Brandon had turned the tables on her. She had started talking to draw him out and had ended by telling him all about herself.

They fell silent as they traversed the long, winding street that led to Wickart-on-Sea, and soon they were following the twists and turns that led into the village. Lord Brandon withdrew his handkerchief and held it to his nose.

"I wish," he complained, "that it did not stink of fish."

What else did he expect of a fishing village? "We are almost there, for Mrs. Amber lives not far from Cully Horris. But what is this?"

Colonel Howard, on a mettlesome bay, sat waiting by the hawthorn hedge that edged Cully Horris's garden. Behind him, like a phalanx of foot soldiers attending their general, were a dozen of his tenants, all of whom were armed with staves and pistols. Two of these retainers were questioning Cully, who stood in front of his closed door.

"Wonder why Captain Hackum is payin' a visit," remarked Lord Brandon idly.

It was plain that Cully did not care for the visit. His arms were folded across his chest, and he kept shaking his head. As they approached, Cecily could hear him say, "An Henglishman's 'ome is 'is castle. You 'ave no right to go in there."

"Then you admit that you have something to hide," suggested the colonel.

The young man shook his head vehemently. "I hain't suggesting no such thing—your honor."

"Then why will you not allow my men to search your house?" Howard demanded.

"What right does he have to search anyone?" Cecily wondered, indignantly. "He is not an officer of the law."

Cully was protesting, "I told you why you wasn't being hinvited in. T' lad is sick."

"That's a likely story." Leaning forward in his saddle, the colonel stabbed an accusing finger at the fisherman. "My Riders have been observing you, Horris. Last night you were seen driving a cart up to and away from Robin's Cove. My Riders tried to detain you, but you got away."

Cully said nothing, and Howard nodded to his retainers. "Ableman, you and Pruett lead a search into the house."

"Infamous!" Cecily exclaimed. But as she started forward, a hand clamped itself about her arm.

"Let it be," Lord Brandon said.

"Who are you to give me orders?" she blazed up at him. She tried to shake loose his hand, but Lord Brandon's fingers were like steel. "Let me go at once," she commanded him. "That man is a bully, and—*will* you let me free!"

Lord Brandon held her fast. Outraged and helpless, Cecily heard Cully's voice rise in protest. "My son *is* sick. I was set ter go to Marcham Place to get some medicine from 'er ladyship.''

"Here I am," Cecily cried. As all eyes turned to her, she held up her basket of herbs. "I have a special decoction here for Tim Horris's putrid throat. Putrid throat," she added significantly, "is highly contagious."

The rank and file paused uneasily, and the one called Ableman said, "Perhaps, sorr, we houghtn't to disturb the lad."

Colonel Howard said something that sounded like *"Tchah."* He dismounted, flung his reins at his nearest henchman, and strode over to confront Cully. "So your boy is sick, is he?" Suddenly he raised his riding crop and brought it down on the young man's shoulders. "You are a liar as well as a criminal," he shouted.

"Shame!" Cecily cried.

Then she turned upon Lord Brandon. "And shame to you, too. Why do you not stop this?"

"I never interfere in other people's business when I can help it," was the cool reply.

He was contemptible. Cecily tore free of Lord Brandon's grasp, caught up her damp skirts, and ran toward the cottage crying, "Stop beating that man!"

The colonel did not even bother to turn his head. "This is no place for a woman," he rasped. "This business does not concern you."

With the whip in his fist, he looked deadly, but Cecily was too angry to be intimidated. "Indeed, it is my concern," she retorted. "If you do not stop at once, I will call the watch."

The colonel's only answer was to raise his crop again. Cecily started forward with some intention of arresting that blow but was shouldered aside. "Now, what's this?" drawled Lord Brandon.

As leisurely as though he were inspecting his breakfast, he strolled forward and examined Cully through his quizzing glass. "What's the fellow done?"

"I have no time to explain to you," the colonel gritted. "Stand back."

Once more he raised his arm. Simultaneously Lord Brandon leaned forward, and the colonel's riding crop raked the front of his jacket. Lord Brandon started as the whip end of the colonel's crop tore off one of his huge brass buttons.

"Hi," Brandon shouted, "confound it, Howard. See what you've done to my coat!"

"I told you to move back, didn't I?" But the colonel's snarl turned to a bellow of outrage as Lord Brandon seized his whip hand and twisted it behind his broad back.

"I *said*," Lord Brandon repeated, "look what you've done to my coat!"

His voice was almost petulant. "You've knocked off one of my buttons into the mud. Not any button, mind, but my own special invention. I had to hunt all over London to find a craftsman skilled enough to make 'em, and he destroyed the design. I tell you, they are unique. Prinny himself would give his soul for that button that you knocked into the mud."

"Damn you, let me go." Howard attempted to extricate his whip hand but found he could not move. Cecily watched in astonishment as the shorter, slighter Lord Brandon easily held the giant colonel prisoner. "Leave go of me or you'll be sorry," the colonel threatened.

"Not until you apologize," the duke's son said.

"Until I—! I'll do no such thing," the colonel retorted furiously. "You got in my way, damn you. You had no right—"

"Seems to me," Lord Brandon interrupted, "that *you* had no right beatin' this fellow here. This is England, and that's truth. You can't go around thrashin' people for no reason. Not ton at all. Settin' yourself above the law, that's what you've been doin', you and your henchmen."

The rank and file were looking uneasily at each other. They shifted from foot to foot and looked longingly at their horses as Lord Brandon continued, "If you think Horris has contraband in his house, bring the watch and let *them* search."

The colonel let loose a stream of oaths. His face had turned almost magenta, and he glared at Cully and at Lord Brandon, who drawled, "Temper, Colonel. A soldier has to control himself, remember."

"Let me go," the colonel snarled, "or I will tear your head off."

With a sigh, Lord Brandon nodded. "You heard him," he said to the world at large. "He's sworn at me. Called me names. Ruined my *coat.* There's nothin' for it but to demand satisfaction, sir."

The colonel was about to open his mouth to roar that he would gladly put a bullet through the effete dandy, then realized that the grip on his arm was like steel. Though Brandon might smell like a Bond Street fribble, he had somewhere acquired a formidable strength of arm.

And there was something even more disturbing. If he quarrelled with Pershing's disgusting son, he might well have to deal with the father. The Ice Duke could be a formidable adversary, and though Colonel Howard scorned the man's pacifistic ideas in regard to America, he had no desire to have open warfare with him.

With a stupendous effort he controlled himself and growled, "You're the one who interfered with me."

"Then *you* can demand satisfaction," Lord Brandon replied promptly. "Delighted, 'pon my honor. Who's actin' as your seconds?"

"Nobody, damn it. There's no need for a duel. You don't hand a man your cartel because of a frumpery button—"

"A button *and* my coat. Look at the mess you've made of it."

Lord Brandon let go of the colonel, stepped back, and turned his back on him. After glowering at that back for a moment, the colonel bent down and retrieved the button from the mud. "Will this content you?" he snarled. "Here, take the filthy thing. Why aren't you taking it?"

"Because it *is* a filthy thing," drawled the duke's son. "Wipe it first."

The colonel's face became mottled. On the point of throwing the button into Lord Brandon's face, he once again recalled the Duke of Pershing. "Pruett," he roared, "give me a cloth."

One of the rank and file scuttled forward. The colonel wiped the huge button and almost threw it at Lord Brandon. "Will that content you?" he fairly gargled.

Lord Brandon took the button and examined it critically. "I still think that I require satisfaction. My coat—"

"Oh, Beelzebub fly off with you and your coat!"

The colonel strode to his horse, flung himself into the saddle, and galloped off. A few seconds later he and his retainers had vanished around a hairpin bend in the road.

"Well," Cecily was beginning, when there was a splintering crash, followed by a scream.

"God almighty!" Cully exclaimed. "What's that?"

Followed by Lord Brandon, he was off at a run. Cecily, running, too, turned the corner of the road and saw that a cart lay on its side. Nearby in the dirt lay an old man.

"How badly is he hurt?" she cried.

Cully Horris, kneeling by the motionless form, made answer. "I don't know, miss. 'E hain't moving."

"The old man came straight for me—I had no time to move aside." Colonel Howard and his retainers were sitting their horses some distance away. "It was his fault," the colonel accused. "He came around that bend without warning."

"An' hif you wasn't in such a pother, you'da 'eard 'im coming," Cully retorted. "This 'ere is Linus 'Arding, what lives across the way from us. Poor, 'armless old sod."

Kneeling beside the old man, Cecily saw that there was a vicious-looking bruise on his temple and that his leg lay at an odd angle.

"Leg looks broken." Lord Brandon had come to kneel beside her. "That'll mend—it's the head blow I mislike. Cully, go and get me a litter so that we can carry him to your house."

The fisherman ran off. "Horris's house is a few steps away," the colonel objected. "What do you want a litter for?"

"He must be moved as little as possible." Lord Brandon turned to the rank and file. "You—Ableman, isn't it?—help to carry the litter. You, Pruett, go for the doctor. And you, yes you! ride to Marcham Place and beg Lady Marcham to come."

The colonel's retainers started to obey, then stopped and glanced fearfully at their chief, who nodded wordless agreement. His mind was obviously on other things, for when Cully arrived with a flat plank of wood, Howard said, "I'll come with you."

Cecily guessed that no humanitarian instinct had

prompted the offer. Once inside the Horris house, the colonel meant to search for contraband. She glanced uneasily at Lord Brandon, but he was helping to lift the old man onto the makeshift litter.

"Do as you will," he said indifferently, "just don't get in my way."

Howard frowned. He disliked Brandon's tone, but he also realized that he stood on shaky ground. "I didn't see him coming," he growled uneasily. "I had no intention of having anything like this happen."

Lord Brandon did not bother to reply. He was busy giving orders. Cully's wife was set to boiling water. Cully himself was sent to find wood for splints.

"What shall I do?" Cecily asked.

Brandon could not help smiling into her anxious face. "If you'll hold the compress to his temple, it may make him more comfortable. Don't worry, it will all come to rights."

"He is still unconscious," Cecily pointed out.

"He was thrown out of his cart with some force, remember. Luckily he's a tough old fellow. Barring shock, he'll come to and be none the worse for it."

He removed his coat and tossed it aside before starting to set the old man's leg. He exuded confidence with every movement, and Cecily, who chanced to glance at the colonel, saw that he was watching the duke's son with growing suspicion. He, too, had seen beneath the mask of the dandy, Cecily thought, and from henceforth he would watch Lord Brandon carefully. She must warn him for Aunt Emerald's sake.

Pruett now returned with news that the doctor was not at home and would not return before dark, but shortly thereafter Lady Marcham arrived in her trap. Accompanying her on horseback were both Montworthy and Captain Jermayne. Dickinson the underfootman, laden with jars of medicine, rode with Lady Marcham.

She paused only to wash her hands in hot water before examining the old man. "You have seen to the head wound and set the leg, I see. Well done. Now help me give him something to offset shock."

From her place by the sickbed Cecily watched the interaction between her Aunt Emerald and Lord Brandon. She glanced at the colonel to see if he, too, was watching, but Howard had wandered off. Assisted by Montworthy and trailed by Captain Jermayne, he had begun to poke about Cully's small cottage.

Montworthy's actions did not surprise Cecily, but she wondered why Captain Jermayne was joining in the unlawful search. But perhaps he was only curious. "Smugglers, eh?" she heard him saying. "Well, it's possible, I suppose. What with the war and all. Dorset's the perfect place for it. By Jove, yes."

Just then old Linus opened his rheumy eyes and demanded to know what had happened and why his head ached like a blacksmith's anvil. Cully explained, and Lady Marcham said that she would remain behind to show Cully's wife how to take care of the old man.

"Trevor, take the trap and Cecily and go back to Marcham Place," she instructed. "Cecily, I will need bistort in case the head wound becomes purulent, and a decoction of lavender for a disinfectant. Get them from the stillroom and send them here with one of the servants. I shall keep Dickinson here in case I need him."

Colonel Howard came up to them. "So the old man will recover?" he demanded.

Lady Marcham did not deign to reply, but Brandon nodded. "Fortunately for you. Be careful that

115

your zeal for ferretin' out smugglers doesn't put you on the wrong side of the law."

"I don't need any warning from you." Colonel Howard paused to add significantly, "I didn't know you were studying to be a sawbones, Brandon."

"Lord, no." Deliberately his lordship donned the coat he had cast off, flicked lint from his cuff, and removing his scented handkerchief, fluttering it under the colonel's nose. "I merely remembered some battlefield doctorin'. In the heat of the moment, you might say."

"That's right," Captain Jermayne interposed. "Had to know some doctoring where we were."

"Where was that—on your way to dinner?" Montworthy sneered. He had noted the attention Miss Vervain was paying to that smatterer, Brandon, and he did not like it at all.

Captain Jermayne blinked hard, but before he could speak, Lord Brandon gave a yelp.

"Dinner! I have actually forgotten about lunch. No wonder I've been feelin' faint. And I quite forgot my, er, damp garments. Your servant, Lady M., gentlemen. Come, Miss Verving, come, before I catch a chill."

He caught Cecily by the elbow and steered her through the door and to the waiting trap. "This time, I will drive," he informed her. "Lunch awaits, and I don't want it to become too impatient."

Cecily remained silent until they had left the house behind. Then she said, "The colonel knows who you are and what you are doing here."

"Does he indeed?" Lord Brandon flicked the reins lightly over the horses' backs. "And what might that be?"

She said it as bluntly as she could. "He thinks you are a smuggler."

Brandon began to whistle softly. Cecily gave him

an exasperated look. "Is that not what you are?" she demanded.

"If it pleases you," he replied cheerfully, "I am a smuggler. I have been called much worse names, believe me. My father, when the mood was on him, would refer to me as a jacknapes, a chitty-faced runt, a—"

"Will you be serious?" Cecily shouted. "You are in danger of being arrested."

"And that worries you?" Looking up at the black eyes that smiled into hers, Cecily felt a sense of imbalance. It was almost as though she were being drawn into their dark depths. She forgot to be angry, forgot Linus's lying unconscious and the suspicion in the colonel's eyes. She heard only the song of the blackbirds and drew in the magical scents of summer.

When she sat there looking at him with that expression in her eyes, Brandon's best intentions began to take French leave. "That is kind," he told her softly. "It means that you must care what happens to me."

His voice was like a caress. Like a moth drawn to fire, Cecily leaned toward Lord Brandon. But as he bent toward her, his steady hand on the reins changed pressure, and the horse threw up its head and neighed.

The noise startled them both. Cecily was aware of the various emotions that were coursing through her and was both angry and a little frightened. Why should Lord Brandon make her feel like this? More to the point, why did she allow herself to be gulled by this devious lord?

"Do not flatter yourself. It means nothing of the kind," she exclaimed fiercely. "I am worried about Aunt Emerald, not you. Have you ever thought what would happen to her if that colonel and his friends arrested you? She could be named your accomplice and arrested, too. Her estates would be confiscated by the crown. She would—"

She broke off as Lord Brandon reached out and covered her hand with his. "Nothing like that will happen," he promised. "I give you my word."

His fingers were cool and strong. They evoked memories she did not care to examine. Jerking her hand away, Cecily cried, "How can you be sure?"

"I would never allow harm to come to her. Or to you."

He thought that she was afraid for herself. Cecily's bosom heaved with indignation, but she did not trust herself to speak. Lord Brandon, she was well aware, could twist her words around so that they came to mean something else.

Turning her head away, she maintained an icy silence as they drove back to Marcham Place. There she requested, in frozen tones, that he set her down on the garden path.

"Goin' to the herb garden without waitin' for lunch? Now, that's true heroism," Lord Brandon opined.

Not waiting for him to help her down from the trap, Cecily dismounted and walked very quickly down the path that led to the herb garden. Well, she told herself, she had warned him. It was more than he deserved. If Colonel Howard caught him and sent him to prison, it would serve him right . . .

Her thoughts were checked as, in the periphery of her vision, she glimpsed a flash of color. She turned her head quickly. Though the herb garden was silent and deserted, the branches of the trees just behind the statue of Ceres were moving gently.

There was no wind. Something—or someone—had just disappeared into the woods.

And that someone had not wanted to be seen.

Cecily stopped short as she considered that the colonel was all abroad in searching Cully's house. She would lay odds that whatever he was seeking lay hidden in the Haunted Woods.

Chapter Eight

It had rained all morning, and the afternoon skies were still heavy with moisture. A fitful wind tugged at Cecily's skirts as she walked briskly through the herb garden. Lady Marcham was occupied in the house, and Lord Brandon was pretending to doze in a corner. It was the perfect moment to explore the woods.

"Miss Vervain! Your most obedient, ma'am!"

Cecily's heart sank as she saw James Montworthy striding toward her. He was dressed for riding and carried a crop in one gloved fist. "Just arrived with the pater and Jermayne," he said. "Lady Marcham said that you had gone out walking. Give you m'word, ma'am, it's been a long time since we met."

He spoke as though he was sure that she had been pining for his attentions. Cecily remained repressively silent as he continued, "Heard that Harding's on the mend. Talk in the village is that you and Lady Marcham have been taking care of him. Think it commendable myself. Always said it was a good thing to be kind to the lower orders."

His condescension was almost as bad as the colonel's. "I am glad that we meet with your approval," Cecily said coldly. "Now, if you will excuse me, I must continue my walk."

"Hoped I could persuade you to ride out with me," Montworthy suggested. "Got my team of grays out front."

"Thank you, but I have not the time," Cecily said.

"Perfect day for it. Whip around the woods, rattle up to the Widow's Rock—show you what my high-steppers can do." As Cecily turned her steps toward the house, Montworthy added, "You don't want to go in there. Jermayne's droning on and on about the war, and Brandon's asleep. The pater's nattering about an apricot fool that he tasted at Lady Hanson's turtle supper. He's the biggest fool, but he don't see that."

He paused to laugh at his own wit, and Cecily said, "I beg you will excuse me, Mr. Montworthy."

Her dismissive tone finally got through to him. "Have you got your bristles up about that argle-bargle in the village?" he demanded. "Old hunks getting hit in the noodle? Not my fault, Miss Vervain—wasn't even there. Fact is, that fellow Harding ran smack into the colonel. Not Howard's fault, is it, if a fool runs into him?"

Cecily said sharply, "The old man was nearly killed because Colonel Howard lost his temper."

A contemptuous look hardened Montworthy's eyes. "Brandon's enough to make anyone get on his high ropes. Give you m'word on it, it's hard to believe he's the Ice Duke's son. Should tell him so one day."

"I doubt," Cecily retorted, "whether your good opinion would count with Lord Brandon."

The Corinthian frowned at the tone of her voice, then reminded himself that he must not brangle with the pretty country mouse.

"Let's talk about other things," he suggested.

"I have no time to talk at all. Excuse me, for I must be going." Cecily started to move away, but he blocked her path. "I beg that you will step out of my way," Cecily exclaimed.

There was an odd note in her voice, and James hid a smile. He was certain that Miss Vervain was merely playing a game with him. He had played variations of it in London with ladybirds and straw damsels as well as respectable females, and he knew where the wind sat.

Putting a coaxing hand on her arm, he lowered his voice to a seductive murmur. "Don't go. If you knew just how beautiful you are just now—"

He was interrupted by a growl that raised the hair on the back of his neck. Looking around, Montworthy saw a cat glaring at him.

"Archimedes thinks you are harming me," Cecily warned. "You know what he is like. You had better back away from me—slowly."

Like an avenging fury, Archimedes began to pad forward. His tail was swollen to twice its normal size, and his lips were pulled back to reveal his one tooth. James retreated, holding his riding crop in front of him.

"Put your crop down. It will only goad him to— Archimedes, stop it at once. Oh, be careful!"

As Cecily cried out, Montworthy stumbled over a rake that had been left in the herb garden. He tried to regain his balance, could not, and fell into a clump of low-growing asparagus fern. Cursing volubly, he tried to rise, but Archimedes had jumped onto his chest. "Get this brute away from me," James shouted, as Archimedes began kneading his victim's shirtfront with his paws.

"Am I interruptin' something?" an interested voice drawled.

Lord Brandon was standing a few yards away and examining the scene through his quizzing glass. "What," he asked, "are you doing among the ferns, Montworthy?"

On this gloomy morning Lord Brandon looked like a burst of sunshine. He wore a canary-colored coat with mother-of-pearl buttons, a striped yellow waistcoat, and mustard-yellow pantaloons. His legs were encased in cream-colored stockings tied with silk ribbons.

"Your father and I have come to an impasse," he continued. "He tried to persuade me that a pinch of marigold in the sauce makes it better. To my mind flowers should stay in the garden and not infiltrate the saucepan. You have to draw the line somewhere."

Cecily was trying to lift Archimedes off James's chest, but the cat had a good claw-hold. "Do not prose on so," she snapped at Lord Brandon. "Help me get this wicked cat away from Mr. Montworthy."

"To hear is to obey." Lord Brandon sauntered closer, bent down, caught Archimedes by the scruff of the neck and gave him a firm shake. "Enough, sir," he commanded.

To Cecily's astonishment, Archimedes meekly let go of Montworthy, who sat up and sputtered, "That brute attacked me. He's dangerous."

He began to get to his feet, then yelped. "My ankle—it's broken. I'll scrag that wretched beast for this."

Brandon pointed out that since the animal had only been protecting his mistress, Montworthy had himself to blame.

"You should have remembered what happened to Howard when he interfered with Miss Verving," he continued. "He's actually as gentle as a lamb."

The "lamb" lay purring in Brandon's arms. When put down, Archimedes rubbed against the lord's leg before swaggering over to do the same to Cecily. He then sat down, eyed James, and licked his chops.

Cecily exclaimed, "You wicked cat, you have hurt Mr. Montworthy."

"What is this you say—oh, *who* has wounded you?"

Delinda Howard had come into the herb garden. Her modish London bonnet was slightly askew over the tight bun at the nape of her neck, and her walking-out dress of ruffled white cambric had all the style of a leg of mutton. "Who has wounded you, Mr. Montworthy?" Delinda repeated.

James glared at Archimedes. "That brute attacked me," he said sullenly. "Made me break my ankle."

"But that is horrible. Poor, *poor* Mr. Montworthy—let me assist you back to the house. Lady Marcham will make things better."

Brushing past Lord Brandon and Cecily, she tenderly took Montworthy's arm and led him away. "Exit unwanted suitor and his devoted handmaiden," Brandon murmured.

"Mr. Montworthy is no suitor of mine," Cecily began, but her lips had begun to twitch. She glanced at Lord Brandon and intercepted such a merry look that she burst out laughing. So did he. They laughed until Cecily's sides fairly ached.

"It is cruel to laugh," she gasped at last. "The poor man was really hurt. I hope he does not insist that Archimedes be destroyed."

"I wouldn't worry about that. No man—especially not one of Captain Hackum's brave Riders—would admit to being routed by a *cat*."

With his breath warm on her cheek, Cecily realized how near to Lord Brandon she was standing.

Under pretext of patting Archimedes, she hastily withdrew from danger.

Brandon watched her with a longing that she did not see. "Lady M. sent me to bring you back to the house," he explained after a moment. "Sir Carolus's conversation has made everyone hungry, so she's called for an early luncheon. Sensible lady, 'pon my honor. The Montworthys and Jermayne were goin' to remain for the repast, but I don't know what they will do now."

However, when they entered the marigold room, they found the Montworthys in no apparent hurry to leave. Sir Carolus was wiping his forehead and sipping sherry. James was stretched out on a Chinese daybed, and Lady Marcham, with Delinda's help, was engaged in bandaging his ankle. Cecily noted that Captain Jermayne, who had withdrawn to stand beside the window, kept his eyes on Delinda.

"I cannot abide the sight of pain," Sir Carolus was saying plaintively.

"Mrs. Horris will be serving duck with lemon-and-raisin sauce," Lady Marcham said briskly. "It will soon put you to rights. Cecily, do ring for Dickinson to take the water and bandages away. And do not fret so, Delinda. No one has yet died of a sprained ankle."

Delinda, who had been looking yearningly at Montworthy, blushed painfully, and Captain Jermayne came to her rescue. "Understandable. I feel as blue as a razor when a friend is hurt," he commented.

A grateful look from Delinda made him stop short, turn bright red, and then go pale under his tan. "I mean to say," he faltered, "that's how I feel. Not how you feel. By Jove, no."

As the captain stammered into silence, Montworthy frowned. He cared not a rush for Delinda, whom he had mentally classified as a tallow-faced antidote unworthy of his attention, but he enjoyed being the center of attention.

Jocosely he said, "Talking about the war again, eh, Jermayne?"

Now that he was not addressing a female, the captain found his tongue again. "Can't help it," he replied. "Always seems to be a war somewhere."

At this Sir Carolus looked anxious. "One has heard that the talks at Ghent are continuing."

"I'm talking about Boney, sir. Bleater's gathering his forces. We'll be needed again, and soon. By Jove, yes." He turned to Lord Brandon. "Sorry you're not going to be in the thick of things? Cannons here, cannons there—"

James began to laugh. "Closest *he'd* come to cannons'd be fireworks, give you m'word. Ain't that right, Brandon?"

The captain looked about to speak but was forestalled by Delinda, who exclaimed, "But that is why I have come." She fumbled with her reticule and drew out an envelope, which she handed to Lady Marcham.

Her ladyship raised her eyebrows in surprise. "But how extraordinary," she exclaimed. "I collect that this is the first time we have been invited to the colonel's estate since he took up residence."

"What's the occasion?" Lord Brandon drawled.

"The colonel writes that his military museum is complete and that he wishes to dedicate it on Friday evening. There will be a picnic supper and a display of fireworks to commemorate the event. What do you think, Trevor?"

Lord Brandon shrugged and said he and the colonel were not exactly the best of friends, whereupon Delinda explained that this was the reason for the invitation. "Neighbors should be friends," she concluded earnestly.

"Well said. If we were all friends, there'd be no wars." Captain Jermayne approved. Then, intercepting another grateful look from Delinda, he retreated into blushing silence.

"The captain is right," Lady Marcham announced. "I am fond of fireworks, and the Brock family, whom the colonel has engaged to manage the display, is well regarded. Besides, Friday will be the dark of the moon, so we will see the fireworks very clear." She paused. "What say you, Trevor?"

Lord Brandon was examining his nails through his quizzing glass. "As long as the man sets a good table," he said indolently, "I am willin' to extend the olive branch."

"And you, my dear?"

Cecily said, "I will do whatever you wish, ma'am."

But she had no desire to go to the Howards'. The colonel had no love for any of them, and especially had he no love for Trevor.

Cecily felt her cheeks grow warm as she realized that she was thinking of the duke's son by his first name. She shot a glance at him, but he was telling Sir Carolus about a display of fireworks he had seen in London.

Shortly thereafter lunch was served. Cecily noted that Captain Jermayne hardly touched his plate, but that both Montworthys did justice to the food. Sir Carolus went into raptures over the wild duck with lemons and praised the potato-and-onion soufflé that accompanied it to the skies.

He implored Lady Marcham to allow him to compliment the cook in person, and when Mrs. Horris appeared, he hopped to his feet and bowed as though she were royalty.

127

"One has partaken of this dish many times, but one has never before encountered such a delicate flavor." Breathing hard, he bent a speaking look on Mrs. Horris. "Tell me, ma'am—how is it done?"

Mrs. Horris blushed and curtsied so profoundly that she nearly collapsed onto the floor. "It's an old family recipe, sir," she twittered. "The secret is in the last fifteen minutes o' cooking. I mix lemon juice and butter and pour the 'ole hover the duck."

The little squire clapped his hands in rapture. "Quite wonderful! One must attempt it at once."

"Not at Montworthy House, you won't. I want to keep our cook," James growled. Obviously humiliated that his sire should stoop so low as to admire a mere servant, he added pointedly, "Anyway, the food don't signify. It's the company—of the fair."

Cecily ignored the speaking look he turned on her and felt desperately sorry for Delinda. Like Captain Jermayne, Delinda had hardly touched her food and looked so unhappy that Cecily was grateful when Lady Marcham said, "Cecily, my dear, would you be an angel and bring me a bottle of dandelion cordial? I collect that it is now ready for table. I would send one of the servants, but you know I prefer them not to enter my stillroom."

Murmuring that she must be returning home, Delinda followed Cecily from the dining room. "I am so sorry, Delinda," Cecily told her. "I would like to box James Montworthy's ears."

"If only there was *something* that would make him love me," Delinda sighed.

Cecily stopped and looked hard at the young woman in her hideous, expensive clothes. "If you mean, is there a love potion, the answer is no," she said frankly. "But there are other ways. Will you come with me to my room, Delinda?"

"Now? But Lady Marcham said—"

"Aunt Emerald will agree that helping you is more important than wine." Shooing Delinda ahead of her, Cecily mounted the stairs and closed the door of her room after them both. "Now," Cecily said, "stand here in the light."

Bewildered but willing to please, Delinda obeyed. Cecily walked around her critically. "Will you unpin your hair, Delinda?" she then asked.

Once more Delinda did as she was told. When the pins were removed, a quantity of pale gold hair came tumbling down, and Cecily exclaimed, "Your hair is beautiful. Why do you crimp it into curls or confine it to that horrid net?"

"It is the fashion," Delinda protested.

"Fashion must wait upon the woman and not the other way around. Oh, Delinda, your eyes are lovely, too, and you have a pretty mouth. The clothes are wrong, that is all."

Delinda looked wonderingly at herself in the glass. Her mother had died very early, and no one else had thought to compliment her. "I do not care for them myself. I should not say that, really—they are very expensive clothes," she murmured guiltily. "Aunt Jane Howard in London picks them out for me—so kind of her, I am sure—when we go to town for the season. Papa says she has superior taste."

If Aunt Jane Howard was anything like the colonel, she must bully Delinda, too. "I am sure she means for the best," Cecily said diplomatically, "but the style she chooses is too old for you."

She went to her armoire and drew out an old dress of hers. It was a thrice-turned damask the color of forget-me-nots. "See how this shade brings out the color of your eyes?" Cecily asked.

Delinda held the dress up to her neck. "I never thought to wear this color before," she murmured.

"Aunt Jane Howard says pastel colors are suitable for me, that I have no town bronze and no sense of style."

Cecily repressed many things she would have liked to say about Delinda's aunt. "I was more fortunate than you," she said instead. "Even after my mother died, I had an old nurse who was an expert seamstress. She taught me a great deal. See, I will explain what I mean."

She drew some sketches, illustrating that clothes with fuller skirts and different necklines were more flattering and that gloves worn to the elbow could disguise thin arms. Next she called upon Mary to dress Delinda's hair.

Like one bemused, Delinda watched herself being transformed. "I do not look the same," she whispered. "I look—oh, *do* you think you can teach my abigail how to dress hair like this, Mary?"

"Sure and I don't see why I couldn't," Mary replied good-naturedly. " 'Tis beautiful hair, you have, ma'am, like moonbeams and mist. You look as radiant as Queen Mab herself."

Intoxicated with these compliments, Delinda did look radiant. "There is a dressmaker in the village," she said eagerly. "Aunt Jane Howard would say that she is provincial, but perhaps—is it possible that you would go there with me, Cecily?"

"Of course I will come." Cecily was almost as delighted as Delinda. "We must have you looking magnificent on the night of the fireworks," she added.

Some of the joy in Delinda's eyes dimmed. "The night of the fireworks," she repeated. "Cecily, there is something I must tell you. Alone."

Wondering at her mysterious tone, Cecily dismissed Mary. "One good turn deserves another," Delinda then said. "I could not help but notice that there is a—a friendship between you and Lord Brandon."

Something deep within Cecily grew suddenly tense. "I would hardly call it that," she parried.

Delinda looked flustered. "Forgive me if I spoke out of turn, but you see, Papa—you know he is determined to stamp out smuggling in Dorset—has suspicions that Lord Brandon is . . . is somehow involved with the smugglers. Do not eat me, Cecily, but that is what he thinks. He has never liked Lord Brandon, and since Linus Harding was injured, his dislike has become hatred. Cecily, why should Papa invite a man he hates to his house?"

It took an effort to smile and say, "Do you stand there and tell me that the colonel is setting a trap for Lord Brandon?"

"Of course I do not know for sure—Papa would hardly confide in *me*—but I have overheard him telling Mr. Montworthy that his net is closing about the smugglers and their leader. He keeps strict watch over Robin's Cove. Perhaps I should not have spoken, but you are my friend—"

Looking distressed, Delinda broke off. Cecily hugged her, told her she was a pea-goose, and that the only one to be trapped was likely to be James Montworthy. "When he sees you transformed, I am persuaded he will be completely dazzled," she said, laughing.

But laughter died as soon as Delinda had gone, and like a pack of hungry wolves, worries began to crowd Cecily's mind. If Delinda guessed right, Lord Brandon could be accused—and arrested—at any moment.

I must warn Aunt Emerald, Cecily thought.

But when she returned to the dining room, Grigg informed her that the Montworthys and Captain Jermayne had departed. Moreover, her ladyship,

131

along with Lord Brandon, had driven into the village to see how Linus Harding fared. "Though," the butler added, "I make bold to say that his lordship did not seem to care for the idea. He protested that it would surely rain."

As she listened to Grigg, Cecily realized that this was a heaven-sent opportunity. She could at last explore the Haunted Woods with no fear of discovery.

"I am persuaded that Lord Brandon is right," she said. "I must finish my walk before it starts to rain."

Outside, the skies were still lowering, and the wind had become brisk. Cecily walked swiftly in the direction of the herb garden. There she paused, only to make sure that she was not being observed, before slipping past the statue of Ceres and into the woods.

Though not at all fanciful, Cecily had to admit that the place had an unusual atmosphere. The breeze had fallen off, and the intertwined trees and bushes seemed to press closer as she walked down the path toward the tumbledown groundkeeper's cottage, where the path ended in a dense thicket of alder trees.

"So now what do I do?" she mused.

Her words ended in a little shriek as something crashed through the thicket toward her. Cecily would have run for her life, but her legs seemed to have gone to jelly. Then she saw Archimedes sitting in the branches of the nearest alder tree, His tail was lashing, his one fang gleaming dangerously.

"You have very near frightened me to death," Cecily scolded. "Have you not caused enough trouble for one day? Come here, sir."

Ignoring her, the cat attempted to leap from one

branch to the other. He almost missed, scrabbled wildly for a claw-hold, and hung on. Then, to Cecily's astonishment, the entire tree to which he was clinging began to collapse sideways.

She went over to examine it and saw that the tree had no root. It had been cut down and stuck into the ground. Judging from the sap that still oozed, it had been cut recently. Cecily tugged sharply at another alder and felt this tree shift slightly. It, too, had no root.

"So," she murmured, "now we will see what his lordship is hiding."

Through the gap that the downed alder had left, she could see the woodland path continue and wind through the trees. Cecily was preparing to step through the opening when she heard footsteps coming toward her.

Lord Brandon! Cecily thought as she hastened to replant the alder tree, but it was not Brandon who appeared on the path but Dickinson. The young underfootman was apparently in a great hurry, for he was almost running.

"What are you doing here?" Cecily demanded.

Dickinson saw her, gaped, and went pale. "M-miss Vervain," he stammered.

Then, to Cecily's astonishment, he fell on his knees in the mud and clasped his hands imploringly. "Don't tell Mr. Grigg on me," he begged. "If 'er leddyship knew I was 'ere, I'd be turned off without no character."

Sternly Cecily repeated, "What are you doing here?"

"I were meeting someone," Dickinson muttered sullenly.

Light dawned. "But Mary is terrified of the woods," Cecily protested.

"That were why." Dickinson hung his head as he

confessed, "We thought—being as she's scared an' all—it would be the last place people'ud think to look for us."

It was not up to her to reprimand Aunt Emerald's servants. Briskly Cecily said, "It were best that you attend to your duties in the future. Get up and go back to the house."

The young man rose and hastened away. As he went, he kept looking back at Cecily as though he were afraid she would change her mind. Something in his furtive manner touched upon a memory, and she realized that it had been Dickinson who had followed Lord Brandon into the woods on the night of Sir Carolus's party.

Was Dickinson a smuggler, too, and in league with the duke's son? For a moment Cecily considered asking Mary but rejected that thought. She doubted if the red-headed abigail knew anything, and even if she did, she would not betray her sweetheart.

Perhaps there were answers on the other side of the false hedge. Once more Cecily parted the alder branches.

"Miss Vervain?"

Grigg was standing behind her, an open umbrella in his hand. "It has begun to rain," he explained.

"That is very kind." While endeavoring to quieten her pounding heart, Cecily looked hard at the elderly servant. Grigg had seen her about to part the alders and step onto the path beyond, but he had also been in her aunt's employ for many years. Surely he could be trusted.

"I have discovered something very odd," she told him. "See here—these alders are not really trees. They have been placed here to conceal this path."

To her surprise she saw that a pale smile had

crossed Grigg's lips. "Begging your pardon, ma'am," he said, "you have stumbled on a fairy fence." Seeing that Cecily looked bewildered, he explained, "The villagers believe that alder branches cut and placed in the ground serve to keep the little people penned up in these woods. I myself," he added hastily, "do not believe in such superstitious nonsense, but the villagers do."

Feeling somewhat foolish, Cecily returned to the house. I am becoming as bad as Colonel Howard and soon will see smugglers under every rock and tree, she told herself. And yet—

And *yet* she could not quite accept Grigg's explanation for the false hedge. It were best, Cecily decided, to tell Aunt Emerald the whole. What her grandaunt did with the information was up to her.

Cecily waited anxiously for Lady Marcham to return from the village, but her waiting was in vain. Her aunt returned too late even to change her clothes for dinner, and once at table, Lord Brandon would not let them have a moment alone. Later, when they left him to his port, Grigg requested a private conference with his mistress about domestic matters, and once more Cecily could not speak.

She prowled about the door of the periwinkle room where Grigg and her ladyship were conducting their interview, and as soon as the butler had exited, she hurried inside the room and said, "Aunt Emerald, I must speak with you. I suspect that Lord Brandon is in league with the smugglers."

Her only answer was a soft snore. Apparently worn out by her long day, Lady Marcham had fallen fast asleep.

So the news would have to wait till morning, Cecily told herself. There was nothing for it but to go to bed, but she felt far too restless to sleep. She dismissed Mary and, instead of undressing, paced her chamber while trying to decide what she should do. "I *should* have spoken earlier," she told Archimedes, who lay sleepily by the hearth. "I should not have waited for proof. I will tell her tomorrow—but tomorrow might be too late."

She walked to her window, opened it, and leaned out to gaze toward the woods. The afternoon's rain had cleared the air, and the night was fine and cool. A sickle moon, fluttering between ragged clouds, threw shadows everywhere. And there by the japonica bushes was . . . no—*yes!*—the shadow of a man striding toward the herb garden.

If she followed Lord Brandon now, she would catch him dead to rights. Cecily paused only long enough to reach for her shawl before she slipped down the stairs and out of the door.

The herb garden was deserted and dark, the woods even darker, but when she reached the groundkeeper's cottage, she could see that one of the alder trees had been taken down.

Beyond the false hedge lay a narrow path. Not pausing to consider the risk she was taking, Cicely stepped through the opening and continued down the path.

As she walked along, the path grew broader and the sound of the sea intensified. Then, above the mutter of the waves, she heard Lord Brandon say, "At the dark of the moon, then."

Cecily stopped where she was and listened intently but heard no answer save an unintelligible murmuring. Cautiously she edged closer. Now the voices were louder and more distinct, and the path broadened into a crossroads. Here a group of men were grouped together.

"Are you sure that it's safe to land?" one of these shadowy men was asking.

His intonation sounded odd, but before Cecily

could decide why, Lord Brandon replied. "Yes. My men will keep Howard busy, don't fear. It'll be safe for our purposes, Major."

"I hope you understand our concern, my lord," the other man said. "After all, this isn't Boston harbor. My men and I are a long way from home."

With difficulty Cecily bit back a cry of horror. No wonder the man's accent had sounded different. He was an American!

She had suspected that Lord Brandon was a smuggler, but the reality was much worse. She now had proof that he was a traitor to his country.

Chapter Nine

Treason.

Cecily felt as though a tight band had been clamped around her chest. Not only was Lord Brandon playing for much more desperate stakes than she had ever imagined but she herself was in danger. She must get back to the house without being seen. But as she stepped backward, her foot crunched down on a twig.

"What was that?" she heard Brandon exclaim.

In the silence that followed, Cecily was sure that the listening men could hear her heart pounding. She held her breath until the American said, "I don't hear anything."

"Probably a rabbit or a deer. Major, nothing will interfere with our plans. Lie off the coast and wait for my signal."

The assurance in Lord Brandon's voice made Cecily's skin crawl. Numb with disgust and horror, she watched the traitor shake hands with the American. There was the sound of receding footsteps, a swish of underbrush, and then silence.

For a long moment Lord Brandon stood listening

to the silence. Then he began to walk back along the path, and Cecily held her breath. She closed her eyes and willed herself not to panic as he passed within a few feet of her. He was going away. She was safe.

A hand covered her mouth, her head was twisted back. "Don't make a sound," a hard voice warned her.

She could not have made a sound if she had wanted to. She could not even catch her breath. "Let's have a look at you," Lord Brandon said. He pushed her ahead of him into the crossroads. There the sickle moon lit her face, and he exclaimed, "Good God."

He let go of her and stepped back to frown down at her. "I should have known that it was you," Lord Brandon sighed.

"How could you betray your country?" she flung at him.

"I'm no traitor."

"Of course you would say that. You are a liar as well, Lord Brandon."

By the moonlight she could see that he had turned pale. "Look into my eyes, and tell me if I lie."

He caught her by the shoulders, but she turned her head defiantly away. "Celia," Lord Brandon said, "look at me."

Cecily's will crumbled. As though obeying an irresistible force, her eyes met his. Though every atom of reason in her brain shouted that Lord Brandon was a turncoat, a sixth sense whispered that his were the most honest eyes she had ever seen.

"Well?" he snapped, "Do you think me a liar and a knave? If you do, you'd better hand me over to the colonel and his brave Riders. Montworthy would enjoy taking me prisoner. Or you could call the watch."

Cecily drew a breath that broke on a sob. "Why are you doing this?"

Her tears were his undoing. Brandon could endure her anger and scorn, but he had no weapons against her pain. The thought that he had reduced her proud spirit to tears was unbearable. Without stopping to think of the consequences, he took her in his arms.

As he held her close against him, Cecily felt as though everything hurtful or sad in the world had vanished forever. She was in Trevor's arms—she was where she had longed to be all this long time. Dazzled with unreasoning joy, Cecily lifted her mouth for his kiss.

The taste of her lips rekindled a slow-burning fire in him, and the flame that had sprung to life almost from the first moment of their meeting blazed up. She was unique, Brandon thought disjointedly, a woman of spirit and sweetness. For such a woman, a man might give up everything he had held dear.

All conscious thought had long fled from Cecily's mind, but there was knowledge that went much deeper than reason or logic. And that knowledge told her that she was in love with Lord Brandon.

That she had found him in treasonous parlay did not matter. That he could be arrested at any moment no longer concerned her. What was important was that they were together at that moment.

They stayed fused together until the air around them seemed to singe. Then, finally, they drew apart and looked at each other in dazed wonder. "Oh, Celia," Lord Brandon whispered. "Do you know what you have done to me?"

He saw her blink hard, saw that apprehension and fear were returning to shadow her eyes. "I'm no traitor, nor am I a smuggler," he told her sternly. "In your heart you know it."

And she did. Though she did not know how or why, Cecily felt sure that he spoke the truth. Perhaps it was because Lord Brandon had saved her from the Widow's Rock. Perhaps it was because he had always been there when she needed him, or because he made her laugh, or because when she was in his arms, the world could tumble into blue ruin for all she cared.

"Besides," he pointed out, "Archimedes trusts me."

"There is that," she agreed.

His firm mouth curved into a singularly sweet smile, and Cecily could not resist reaching out to caress his hard cheek. He turned to kiss her palm, and the warmth of his mouth seemed to travel through her skin and bones and curve about her heart.

"Why?" she pleaded. "Why the disguise, Trevor? I want so much to understand."

For a moment he hesitated. "I can't tell you that," he said at last. "You must take me on trust for a little longer."

Again he bent his lips to hers. Once more the world seemed to cease its turning. But when this kiss was over, Cecily understood the irony of love. It followed no logic, offered no reason for being. It arrived unheralded, uninvited, even unwanted. And once love had laid siege to the heart, there could be no turning back.

"Say nothing to anyone," Brandon was telling her.

"Is that a command?"

He smiled at the flash of her old spirit, and his eyes grew tender. "A request. And when the time comes, when everything looks blackest . . ."

He paused, and she prompted, "What then, Trevor?"

He took her hand, kissed the palm again, and folded her fingers over his kiss. "When things look blackest, let your trust be stronger than your doubt."

"Is there any doubt as to who the best rider is?" Obediently following Delinda's pointing finger, Cecily looked down at the gentlemen who were riding their horses up and down the colonel's riding track. She easily spotted Montworthy, who was dressed in a dove-colored riding coat, skin-tight doeskin breeches, and gleaming Hessian boots that fit his legs to perfection. He looked to be the quintessential Corinthian, as choice a spirit as ever racketed around the streets of London—and he knew it.

Captain Jermayne was also among the gentlemen below, and by contrast to Montworthy appeared almost provincial. He was not wearing regimentals today, and in his drab black coat, tan breeches and beaver hat, he looked unassuming and rather ordinary. But Cecily had noted that in his unspectacular way the captain was a far better horseman than his swaggering companion.

"To my mind, Mr. Montworthy has carried the day," Delinda continued dotingly. "What a pity Sir Carolus has the gout and is indisposed—he would have enjoyed seeing his son's triumph in the races."

Races for the gentlemen were the colonel's idea of entertainment for his guests, who had begun to arrive at three o'clock in the afternoon. They had been first greeted by their host, who, in honor of the occasion, had donned the regalia of his former regiment.

The colonel in battle dress complete with medals, sashes, and ceremonial weapons was a formidable sight, and most of his guests felt somewhat dazed as they were escorted to a viewing pavilion. From this vantage place they could watch the more athletic gentlemen compete in feats of riding.

Ladies in their finery and jewels were quick to take their seats, ply their fans, and applaud the competitors. Those gentlemen who did not care to race congregated to drink wine and to discuss the politics of the day.

In that gathering of scarlet regimentals, brilliant silks and satins, saucy bonnets and hats that were all the fashion, Cecily resembled a dove. Her China crepe, trimmed with a double pleating of ribbon, was a somber gray, and her bonnet was trimmed with a single silk rose.

By contrast, Delinda was vividly attired in a cornflower-blue dress of jaconet muslin and a saucy hat decorated with blue ribbons and forget-me-nots. She was stylish and almost pretty, and her eyes were bright and hopeful as she watched Montworthy. Then, catching Cicely's smile, she blushed and stammered, "But I forget my duties as a hostess—forgive me. You are not eating anything, dear Cecily."

In truth Cecily had not done more than taste of the ample picnic that the colonel had provided. There were plates of cold chicken sliced thin, lamb cutlets, grouse, pheasant, and ham. There were mountains of pickled crab, pickled mushrooms, crayfish in sauce. The sight of so much food had taken away Cecily's already feeble appetite.

"And you are pale. Do you feel down pin?" Delinda was asking anxiously.

Since her meeting with Lord Brandon in the woods, Cecily had felt decidedly down pin. In his arms she had thought that no matter what the appearances might be, she believed in him. Now logic and reason had reasserted themselves. Lord Brandon could be toying with the safety of England. How could she be *sure* that he could be trusted?

Cecily was grateful when Captain Jermayne's arrival cut short such disquieting thoughts. She gave him a friendly greeting and noted that he flushed when he shook Delinda's hand.

"Ah, er, Miss Howard," he stammered. "Your most obedient, ma'am. Look deucedly fine. Blue suits you. By Jove, yes. Mean to say—eh?"

Close up, the rangy young officer looked homelier than ever. His dark hair was windblown, and his scar stood white on his sunburned cheek. The very act of talking to females had apparently discomfited him, and his forehead was beaded with perspiration.

"Deucedly hot," he mumbled. "Mean to say—yes, hot."

He was so obviously embarrassed that Delinda felt a stab of sympathy. All her life she had been made to feel inadequate by those around her, and even though she had dressed so carefully today in her new clothes, Montworthy was not even looking her way. All of this disappointment and heartache made her understand how awkward poor Captain Jermayne must feel.

Forgetting her own shyness, she said, "You are a very good rider, Captain. Is yours a cavalry regiment?"

An eager look came into the captain's eyes. "Kind of you, ma'am. Yes, it is. Nineteenth Mounted Hussars. I'm honored to serve with them. By Jove, yes." He paused, then made a stupendous effort and added, "Fine picnic, ma'am. All your doing, I shouldn't wonder."

Delinda blushed at the compliment and looked down at her feet. The captain, having shot his bolt,

lapsed into abashed silence. Cecily said, "I am looking forward to the fireworks, Delinda. I have never
seen a grand display by the Brock family before.
Have you?"

"No, but I am persuaded it will be very fine—
there is to be a fiery spectacle called the Eruption
of Mt. Etna. It is said to be superb." In her enthusiasm Delinda smiled at Captain Jermayne, who
became very red in the face. "Even Lord Brandon
told me earlier that he is looking forward to the
display."

All afternoon Cecily had avoided looking in Lord
Brandon's direction. She had tried not to think of
him. But just the mention of his name had tumbled
down her resolutions, and everything rushed back—
the night and the whisper of voices, and the terror
and the joy. Perhaps, Cecily thought bleakly, Mary
was right when she said that there was enchant-
ment in those words.

But there might also be treachery. "The dark of
the moon," Brandon had said, and that night there
would be no moon in the sky. Cecily clenched her
hands at her sides and gazed full at Lord Brandon.

The duke's son had dressed entirely in black. He
wore a black tailcoat with pockets in the pleats,
black corduroy knee breeches, and a waistcoat with
black flowers.

In that costume he would easily blend with the
shadows. In a few hours he would melt into the
moonless night to play his dangerous game. And
because of her promise to him she must be part of
that game.

She was not sure that she knew all the rules of
the game. At times Cecily found herself wondering
whether Lord Brandon was merely pretending to
care for her. Not once had he spoken of love, and it
was possible—even likely—that the duke's son was

carrying his masquerade one step further and buying her silence with his kisses.

As if aware of Cecily's thoughts, Brandon looked up, and his eyes locked with hers. *Trust me,* those eyes said.

"My dear?"

Cecily wrenched her eyes away from Lord Brandon and focused on Lady Marcham, who had strolled up to her side. "Look at Delinda and that nice young captain," her aunt was saying. "They are actually talking together, even though they are both so shy that they can hardly rub two words together. I am persuaded that they enjoy each other's company."

She paused and smiled at Cecily. "I have not had the occasion to mention this, but you look lovely today. You remind me of your mother, my dear."

Cecily's eyes filled with tears. They annoyed her. She who had never wept through the ordeal of her father's long illness, she who had been dry-eyed when she learned that she was penniless and forced to earn her bread or do without, now seemed ready to weep at the slightest provocation.

"But," her aunt continued, "you are also troubled. Is Trevor making you unhappy?"

It was difficult to laugh around the knot in her throat, but Cecily managed. "You are a great reader of minds, ma'am, but this time you are far afield. I am not sad at all."

Lady Marcham did not press the matter. Instead, she put an arm around Cecily's waist. "You are my only living blood relation. Beyond that I am sure that you know how fond I am of you."

Once again weak-minded tears gritted in Cecily's eyes. By keeping her promise to Trevor, she could be endangering this dear, good woman.

"If Trevor has done something to distress you,"

Lady Marcham continued, "I beg you will confide in me."

Did Aunt Emerald suspect that her godson's disguise hid a different man? For the hundredth time since learning his dark secret, Cecily opened her mouth to tell her grandaunt all she knew. And for the hundredth time the words that would damn Lord Brandon remained unsaid. The promise she had made to him kept her silent.

"To tell the truth," she hedged, "I am weary of this picnic."

To her relief Lady Marcham agreed. "I am only staying for Delinda's sake. All this food and the posturings of that man in his regimentals—really, it is shocking ton. But, Cecily—"

She paused and regarded her grandniece with a look that seemed to read not only her thoughts but all her tangled emotions. "I will give you one piece of advice that has never failed me," Lady Marcham continued. "In case of a conflict between the mind and the heart, it is wise to listen to the heart. Reason may be clouded, but the heart sees with clear eyes."

She walked away to chat with Delinda and Captain Jermayne, leaving Cecily feeling drained and oddly weak in the knees. Her head ached, and there was a raw feeling under her breastbone. She wanted nothing more than to be alone in a quiet place, but the noisy picnic dragged on. Her only consolation was that James Montworthy was so involved in showing off his riding skills that she was spared his company.

After a while the races ended, and the gentlemen contestants went off to change before joining the other guests. By the time they returned, night had begun to fall, and the colonel called for attention.

"I have asked you to join me on this occasion for

147

a special reason," he declaimed. "Some of you know that for the past few months I have been engaged in building a small museum designed to honor English patriots and warriors. If you'll come with me, I'll show you what I mean."

Trailed by his dutiful guests, he led the way down a path edged by ruthlessly pruned bushes, manicured lawns, and a topiary garden that had been planned and planted with geometric exactitude. At the end of this garden stood the summerhouse, which had been enlarged and converted into a square building flanked by marble statues of Mars and Jupiter.

"Here," declaimed the colonel, "is my small tribute to the arts of war. Enter, my friends."

Obediently the guests trooped into the building and looked about them at walls hung with portraits of the colonel's military ancestors. Busts of heroes throughout the ages were prominently displayed, including a life-size statue of the Duke of Wellington. A Latin inscription, etched in the stone lintel, assured everyone that it was sweet and honorable to die for one's country.

Lord Brandon examined this tag through his quizzing glass. "So," Cecily heard him drawl, "this is a military museum. Most interestin' place, 'pon my honor."

It was also a very depressing place. Cecily pretended to examine a map that detailed one of the colonel's many campaigns and wished that the dedication of the museum could be soon over. Unfortunately it had just begun. The colonel cleared his throat, welcomed his guests, assured them that he did not mean to keep them long, and launched into a speech that lasted for half an hour.

Hands locked behind his back, booted legs planted wide, and with medals winking on his chest, the colonel remembered generals, brave officers, gallant men. He described how the Prince Regent had pinned one of the medals on his chest. He went into intricate details of how the great Wellington had once confided a secret to him. "He said, 'Howard, I know that I can tell you because you are a man of honor whose word can be trusted.' And he was right. To this day that secret is safe with me. If I were put to the torture, it would still be safe," the colonel intoned.

Cecily noted that Lady Marcham wore a glazed expression, and that many of the colonel's other guests were looking definitely sleepy. Another long-winded story, and she herself might—

"I *beg* your pardon, Brandon," the colonel snapped, "am I boring you?"

Caught in midyawn, Lord Brandon protested, "It's the smell of fresh paint. Paint always makes me yawn."

The colonel looked about and realized that half his audience was yawning. He therefore gestured to his servants, who began to circulate with trays of crystal goblets full of champagne.

"We will now drink a toast to England," the colonel announced. "May Britannia ever be great. Long live the king!"

He swallowed his drink at one gulp and hurled his glass to the floor. Montworthy and the colonel's other Riders immediately followed suit.

"The purpose of this museum is not only to honor our heroes but to remind us that England is the greatest country the world has seen," the colonel said. "In order to maintain our position of superiority, we must be ready to make sacrifices. We must also escalate our war with the colonials until they are beaten to the knees. War is inevitable, and we must be victorious!"

One of the colonel's guests, a portly and prosperous-looking baronet, ventured to disagree. "There might yet be a third meeting at Ghent," he pointed out. "Gambier and Bathurst and William Adams may forge a peace with the Americans. Considering the cost of a war, I hope they do."

"Tush, man. Isn't England more important than any trumpery cost?" the colonel demanded scornfully. "We are discussing Britannia's honor."

There was a ripple of agreement, mostly from the colonel's Riders, and the colonel waxed expansive. "After all," he asked, "what price can we put on honor? Even Lord Brandon must agree with me there."

All eyes turned to Lord Brandon, who had folded his arms and was leaning back against a marble bust of Lord Nelson. He shrugged and said, "If you say so, Howard."

"I do say so." The colonel leaned forward and fixed his protuberant blue eyes on the duke's son. "Of course you may share the Duke of Pershing's views and counsel peace at any price."

Cecily realized that the colonel was attempting to goad Lord Brandon into open disagreement, but Trevor only shrugged. "As Kirkwood pointed out just now, war costs—fifty-seven million pounds it took to pay foreign armies to fight in Europe." A ripple of amazement filled the military museum, and Lord Brandon added idly, "England has been at war for twenty-one years. Glorious years, of course."

"Are you mocking me, man?" rasped the colonel.

" 'Pon my honor, I'd not dream of it."

Tapping back a yawn, he began to examine a statue that stood nearby. Howard scowled. He suspected that Lord Brandon was deeply involved with the local smugglers and had wanted to anger him into losing his temper and incriminating himself. But his opponent was too crafty to be drawn. He must have patience and bide his time.

He turned his attention to his other guests but not before Cecily had glimpsed the look on his face. Suddenly she could no longer bear to be in the colonel's company. Careful not to be noticed, Cecily backed out of the colonel's museum into the moonless night.

There she paused, uncertain. Should she return to the viewing stand? Should she wait for Lady Marcham?

"I wish," Cecily muttered, "that the sorry night were over."

"Eh, what's that?" A startled voice exclaimed beside her.

Cecily peered into the dark. "Captain Jermayne," she exclaimed in astonishment. "What are you doing out here? I saw you conversing with Miss Howard and thought you had escorted her to the museum."

The captain drew a deep breath that was almost a sigh. "Not me, ma'am. She went with Montworthy."

So Delinda had had her wish. Feeling very sorry for the captain, Cecily held her peace.

"Fine figure of a man, Montworthy. Corinthian. By Jove, yes. Knows how to talk to females. What the hell—I mean, what could I possibly do? I don't know the first thing about ladies. Especially top guns—I mean, fine ladies like Miss Howard."

This time the captain's sigh was clearly audible. "Miss Howard's not like other fe—ladies. She's . . . she's kind and gentle. She doesn't laugh at a fellow. To give you words with no bark on them, Miss Vervain, she suits me down to the ground. But then,

151

why should she look at me when Montworthy is around?"

He lapsed into morose silence, and Cecily forgot her own troubles to say bracingly, "A handsome profile is not everything, Captain. If I were you, I would go back inside the museum and talk to Delinda."

The captain looked aghast. "But what if Miss Howard doesn't want to talk to me?"

"You will never know that unless you try," Cecily pointed out. "Faint heart never won fair lady, Captain."

Jermayne considered the truth of this. "Never fought shy in an engagement before," he said at last. "By Jove, no." Then he jerked his rangy body to military stiffness, saluted Cecily, and marched back into the colonel's museum.

Not wishing to meet anyone else, Cecily began to walk away from the museum. She followed the garden path and in the topiary garden found a shadowed seat. It was cool and peaceful, and she sat down and waited there until voices indicated that the colonel's guests were returning to the viewing pavilion. Among them, Cecily was glad to note, were Captain Jermayne and Delinda walking together.

She saw Lady Marcham pass and was about to get up and join her, when suddenly a shadow loomed between her and the night sky and a familiar voice asked, "All alone in the dark, Miss Vervain?"

Cecily rose to her feet as Montworthy walked around one of the topiary bushes. "The fireworks are going to begin," he announced. "See you've found a quiet place to watch 'em from. Quiet *and* private."

There was no mistaking the insinuating note in

152

his voice. "I must be going," Cecily said coldly. "Aunt Emerald will want me."

"Lady Marcham's promised to keep Lady Bagge and Mrs. Hovernath company. You don't want to sit next to *them*—pair of muffin-faced griffins. Better stay here with me, give you m'word."

Montworthy hardly bothered to mask the triumph that he felt. He had been right all along about Miss Vervain. The country mouse had played out her waiting game, and now the time was ripe. Why else would she have been waiting for him there in the darkness?

Sliding his arm around her waist, he murmured, "Come, m'dear. No need to be coy, eh? No one will see if you give me a little kiss."

Next moment, he was staggering backward with a hand clapped to his ear. "Touch me again, and I will box the other ear, you loose fish!" Cecily threatened.

James stared at Miss Vervain in disbelief. With her eyes narrowed to slits and her small hands clenched, the country mouse looked more like an outraged lioness. "Now, see here," he began.

"I see very well," Cecily retorted. "You are a care-for-nobody, sir. Now go away. Go *far* away, and do not trouble me again."

Astonished, angry, and shaken, James took himself off. Cecily remained where she was. Her heart was racing as though she had been running, and she had begun to tremble with reaction. "At least," she murmured, "he will never try *that* again. I should have—"

She broke off as she heard footsteps approaching. "Did I not tell you to go away?" she cried, but broke off as Delinda appeared out of the darkness. "I—I thought you had gone on ahead with Captain Jermayne," Cecily stammered.

"The captain is such a kind person. But I . . . I missed another."

Delinda ducked her head and Cecily said with some impatience, "If you mean James Montworthy, he is not worth your regard."

"You do not love people because they are worthy or not," Delinda pointed out. "You love them because you cannot help yourself."

There was no answer to this. Delinda continued, "I have decided to take measures into my own hands. Cecily, do not eat me—I am going to make a love potion."

"But there is no such thing!"

"Yes, there is." Passion filled Delinda's voice. "In that book of herbs that Lady Marcham has, I found a recipe that guarantees love."

She drew a deep breath. "To make the potion I need to wear a white dress and unbind my hair, pluck marigolds and wild verbena at the dark of the moon. I must dance a 'stately measure' as I cull the herbs. If I do this—and I will—my true love will be mine."

She paused to ask hopefully, "Do you know where verbena grows wild hereabouts?"

"No," Cecily replied firmly, "and even if I did, I would not tell you. I have never heard of anything so idiotic. Be sensible, Delinda—."

She broke off as Delinda pounded one small fist into another. "I have been sensible all my life. Oh, Cecily, I do not want to watch other girls marry the men of their dreams and have children—I want to love and be loved. You cannot understand how much I want that."

Her voice faltered into a whisper, and Cecily thought of a moonlit glade and strong arms and a voice that asked for her trust. Who was to say that Delinda was wrong? she wondered. Delinda was only seeing with the eyes of the heart.

Cecily put her hands over Delinda's cold ones and squeezed hard. But before she could speak, there was a thunderous roar and the night sky was emblazoned with color. Cecily and Delinda looked upward and stood transfixed as rockets, saxons, star shells, and Roman candles flung themselves against the darkness.

Delinda put her lips to Cecily's ear and shouted, "We cannot hear each other out here. Come back to the house—we can talk there."

As Cecily followed her hostess, she saw that not everyone was enjoying the fireworks. Their lurid glare clearly showed the colonel's massive form standing on the steps before his house. Just then a horseman came riding up.

"That is one of Papa's Riders," Delinda shouted in Cecily's ear.

Uneasily Cecily watched the man swing down from the saddle and race up the stairs to his chief. She could not hear what was being said, but the fireworks lit the colonel's face, and Cecily bit her lip when she saw the expression on his face. Colonel Howard looked like a pit bull who had scented blood.

Trevor, she thought.

There was a lull in the boom and blast of the fireworks, and she heard the colonel ask, "You're certain that the smugglers are carrying contraband?"

His Rider nodded. "A ship was sighted off Robin's Cove. We waited and watched, and soon Horris and a half a dozen others drove carts down to the cove. Half an hour later they left with their carts loaded and began to drive them out of Dorset." The colonel's Rider paused to add gleefully, "This time, sir, we've got them dead to rights."

Chapter Ten

By the red glare of the fireworks, Cecily saw triumph suffuse the colonel's face. "Who is the leader of the pack?" he demanded.

"A man in black," was the reply. "He's taking the road toward the western downs."

"Man in black—that's Brandon right enough," the colonel exulted, and Cecily realized that she had not seen Lord Brandon come out of the colonel's military museum.

She gave Delinda's arm a shake. "Fetch Aunt Emerald for me," she begged. "Please, Delinda. It is most urgent."

Then she picked up her skirts and ran up the stairs toward the colonel calling, "Colonel, I have been searching for you."

"Miss Vervain." Impatience warred with Howard's habitual air of condescension. "I am sorry, but I cannot stay to converse with you."

Determined to keep him from pursuing Lord Brandon, Cecily cast about her mind for some convincing lie. "Aunt Emerald desires to—to consult

157

you immediately on a most important matter," she said.

She was interrupted by a roar, as if a hundred cannons had gone off at once. The colonel's house shook, the windows rattled, and Cecily felt jolted to her bones. She stared up at the sky, which was lit by an unholy glow, and when she looked down again, she saw Delinda and Lady Marcham coming up the path. They were followed by Captain Jermayne.

Delinda was speaking, but Cecily could not hear a word until she reached the steps. "The volcano has just exploded," Delinda was saying. "Such a spectacle—Papa, why are you not watching the fireworks? Your absence was remarked."

"Make my excuses, girl. I have business to attend to."

"But, Papa," Delinda protested, "you cannot abandon our guests."

"In matters such as this, speed is of the essence." The colonel seemed to grow in stature and appear even more formidable. "The smugglers have made their move."

To Cecily's astonishment Captain Jermayne exclaimed, "Now, that's interesting. By Jove, yes. Never thought I'd see smugglers in the flesh. I'd like to ride along with you, Colonel."

The colonel showed his teeth in a grin. "My riders will be glad of your company. And your friend Lord Brandon—perhaps he would also like to join us?"

Cecily's heart sank, but Lady Marcham said, "You are joking, of course. Trevor hates to ride at night. The rogue has gone inside the house, and I strongly suspect that he is taking a nap."

The colonel looked even more pleased with himself. "He is not in the house, Lady Marcham. I have been standing here ever since we left the military museum, and I did not see him." He turned to the Rider who had brought him the news and ordered, "Alert the others, Farmington. And see if you can unearth Lord Brandon."

As the Rider hurried off, Lady Marcham exclaimed, "It is useless to try and persuade Trevor to go with you. He has no interest in smugglers."

"You are far afield, ma'am, far afield. I would say that he is very much interested," the colonel purred. "If I do not mistake, he is leading his band of smugglers from Robin's Cove to the western downs."

Lady Marcham began to laugh. "You are joking me."

"Lady Marcham, I never joke."

"Then you are foxed," she retorted. "Or mad," she added as an afterthought.

Just then Montworthy came striding up the walk. There was a suspicious red mark on his cheek, and he avoided looking at Cecily as he announced, "Brandon's nowhere to be found. Nobody's seen him, neither. Looks like he did a bunk."

"Mount up," the colonel ordered.

Helplessly Cecily watched as the colonel's Riders called for their horses and arms. Her brain had apparently gone numb, for she could not think what she should do. She could only look on helplessly as the colonel buckled on his sword and added a brace of pistols.

James Montworthy was also settling a sword around his waist. "Always thought that fribble Brandon was up to no good," he commented.

"Hold your tongue, sir!" Lady Marcham exclaimed. "Be careful what you say. Pershing will not stand idly by and let his son be slandered." Then turning from the abashed James to the colonel, she added coldly, "I collect that you are accusing my godson of being a common smuggler."

"Not at all common, ma'am," Howard fairly crowed. "He is a prince amongst smugglers. He has brains, but he could not gull *me*. I knew all along that he was gallow's bait."

The insult loosened Cecily's frozen tongue. "If Lord Brandon were here," she cried, "he would shoot you for that insult."

The colonel smiled indulgently. "It is a good thing you are a woman," he said. "If you were a man—"

"If I were a man, you would not dare to take that tone with me," Cecily retorted. "How dare you blacken a gentleman's name when he is not here to defend himself? Besides, you have not one shred of proof."

"I'll have all the proof I need as soon as we see what's in those carts." The colonel strode down the stairs to his waiting horse and swung into the saddle. Then, followed by a score of Riders and a small army of his hastily mustered tenants, he cantered away.

Lady Marcham turned to Delinda. "Be so good as to summon my carriage," she said haughtily. "I will not remain in this house another moment."

Delinda looked ready to burst into tears. "Oh, Lady Marcham, I am so sorry."

"Well, well, I suppose that it is not your fault that your father is a jackass," Lady Marcham said in a milder tone. "Do not cry, Delinda; I am not angry at you."

Just then Captain Jermayne cantered by on his horse. Cecily glared after him. "I thought," she said bitterly, "that he was Trev—Lord Brandon's friend."

"There are friends and friends," Lady Marcham replied cryptically.

"I hope he may fall off his horse," Cecily cried.

Of all the events of the night, the captain's defection bothered Cecily the most, for it illustrated a point most clearly: now that he stood accused of wrongdoing, Lord Brandon had no friends.

Cecily tried to believe that Trevor was miles away and safe, but she could not make the picture. As she followed Lady Marcham into the carriage, her mind conjured up details of the chase, of the colonel's catching up to the smugglers, the flash of swords and the bark of pistols.

"Stop worrying," commanded Lady Marcham. "There is nothing to fear."

Cecily rounded on her. "Nothing to fear! Aunt Emerald, the colonel's riders are armed with swords and pistols. If he resists, they will kill him."

"It is all part of the plan."

Lady Marcham looked about the closed carriage and lowered her voice. "You may be sure that Trevor has no dealings with smugglers. Hush, now. These matters cannot be discussed on the open road."

With difficulty Cecily restrained the questions that crowded her tongue. The short journey to Marcham Place had not seemed so long before. When they were climbing the steps to the house, she could no longer keep from crying, "Tell me this, at least—do you know about the Americans?"

Before Lady Marcham could reply, Grigg opened the front door. Though he was much too well trained to show any emotion, Cecily could swear that there was a glint of annoyance in the butler's eyes.

"M'lady," he announced, "There has been a—an occurrence during your absence."

He lowered his voice and murmured something that Cecily could not catch. Lady Marcham exclaimed, "On this night of all nights? Could you not have prevented—but of course, you could not. We must deal with things as they come, Grigg."

"Yes, m'lady. Also, I regret to say that Mary Tierney has gone mad."

"Mary?" Cecily gasped. "But when I last saw her, she was perfectly sane."

Lady Marcham rolled her eyes. "Send her into the marigold room, and I will see what can be done," she said with a sigh.

"It must be some mistake," Cecily protested as, temporarily diverted from Lord Brandon's troubles, she followed her grandaunt. But when Mary stumbled into the room, she had to admit that the girl definitely had a wild look. She was ghost-pale, and her linen cap was set askew on her red head.

"What on earth ails you?" Lady Marcham exclaimed.

"Sure, and they're *not* of this earth," the girl moaned. "My lady, the little people have landed at the Widow's Rock."

Lady Marcham pushed an impatient breath through her nose. "You were dreaming."

Mary shook her head so hard that her red curls bounced. "Holy saints, wasn't I awake entirely, and standing by the Widow's Rock when I saw the little people coming in from the sea?"

"I suppose you were meeting Dickinson at Widow's Rock?" Lady Marcham asked.

Mary burst into tears. "I didn't go to do so, m'lady. Cook had sent me to get some eggs from the henhouse, and I saw Mr. Dickinson slipping out the gate and down the road that leads ter the sea. An' I thought that if I met him by chance—" She broke off whimpering, "Sure and I ran so hard home, I broke all the eggs, and Mr. Grigg said as I was a wicked girl for trying to meet with Mr. Dickinson, and that you'd turn me off without no character."

"I will do no such thing," Lady Marcham soothed. "Stop crying, you goose. You must have seen fireflies or Saint Elmo's fire on the water."

Mary fell on her knees and called on the blessings of all the saints to fall on Lady Marcham. Then she added, "But it wasn't fireflies, m'lady. Fireflies don't talk amongst themselves, do they? I heard them say they were going to meet in the Haunted Woods." She began to sniffle loudly. "Oh, musha, musha, it's like me mam told me onct—the little people have come to dance about their queen, and me that saw them will be taken away to Fairyland."

Cecily glanced at Lady Marcham and saw an odd expression flicker in her eyes. For a moment she seemed to hesitate. Then she glided forward and placed a hand on the girl's forehead. "As I thought, gadding about after dark has brought on a fever. You have been hallucinating, my girl. Not another word from you, or you will end in a madhouse, not Fairyland. Come to the stillroom with me now, and I will give you a soothing draft."

Subdued by these words, Mary followed Lady Marcham out of the room, but Cecily remained where she was. She was sure that the 'little people' Mary had seen were Americans landing on English soil, and she strongly suspected that Lady Marcham knew of their arrival.

Once more the thought of treason rose blackly in Cecily's mind, and she was now doubly afraid. There were only two people she cared for in the world, and both of them were most probably traitors to the crown. "What do I do now?" she said with a sigh.

A gruff meow at her feet made her look down.

Archimedes was sitting there. Needing to hold something, she bent down and picked him up, and for once he allowed her to stroke him. "What shall I do?" Cecily asked the cat.

Archimedes purred and rubbed his battle-scarred head against her chin, and Cecily pressed her cheek against his rough fur. She envied her cat. His loyalties, like his life, were simple. Because he loved her, he would defend Cecily to the death. The rest of the world, except for a carefully chosen few, could go hang for all Archimedes cared.

Suddenly the cat stiffened in Cecily's arms. His head rose, his whiskers cocked into an alert position, and he glared into the dark. Following the direction of that stare, Cecily saw that a man was walking past the window and into the garden. His back was to her, but she recognized that swift, commanding walk.

"I thought he was riding for the western downs," she gasped.

Archimedes growled, deep in his throat, and with that sound everything came clear to Cecily. She, too, cared less than a rush for the world. She had the greatest affection for Lady Marcham. She loved Trevor. He had told her that when she doubted the most, she must trust, and if ever there was a time for trust, it was now.

"I must warn him," she said aloud. "He may not know that the colonel is on his trail. He *cannot* know that even Captain Jermayne has joined the enemy."

Setting the cat down, she went into the hall. No one was there, and no one saw her open the door and slip outside. There was no sign of Lord Brandon, and in the faint starlight the woods at the edge of Lady Marcham's property looked dark and menacing.

Moving as swiftly as she dared to in the starlit dark, Cecily traversed the herb garden, passed the statue of Ceres, and entered the woods. There the faint starlight did not penetrate, and the darkness was almost absolute. Cecily was groping her way along the path when a dark figure barred her way.

It was not Lord Brandon. This man was taller, heavier, and much more menacing. As Cecily retreated a step, he threw out a hand and caught her by the wrist. "Who are you, and what are you doing here?" he demanded.

His was not an American voice. It was also the coldest, most inflexible voice she had ever heard, and his grip on her wrist was iron-hard. Cecily had never felt so afraid in her life, and it took all the courage she had to command, "Let go of me at once."

"Not until I am satisfied that—blast and confound you, woman, you will *not* faint."

Cecily had pretended to go limp in her captor's grip. When she felt that clasp slacken, she jerked herself free and, picking up her skirts, started to run. He lunged after her and caught her arm, but she kicked back at him with all her strength. Apparently her kick connected, for he gave a muted roar of pain and let her go.

Where was Trevor? Cecily's heart hammered like a kettledrum. Though her eyes had adjusted to the darkness, it was impossible to see the path over which she ran. Suddenly another figure stepped out of the trees before her. "Stay where you are," the newcomer hissed.

Mindlessly Cecily turned to run back the way she had come. Her assailant was too fast. The scream that had been forming on her lips died into a little whimper as he caught her around the neck. "Don't you make a sound, or you'll be sorry," Dickinson snarled.

Acting instinctively, Cecily dug her elbows backward. The underfootman had not expected fight and was caught off guard. He gave a grunt of pain and released her, but a moment later he had recovered and was after her, catching up to her at the edge of the woods. "No bloody fear you'll get away."

The vicious tug he gave her hair nearly snapped her neck. With no strength or breath to cry out, Cecily found her arm gripped and cruelly twisted. Then, letting go of her hair, Dickinson clamped that hand over her mouth.

"Come to warn Lord Brandon, 'ave you?" he sneered. "The colonel's got 'is nibs dead to rights. A common smuggler 'e is, and both you and 'er ladyship is in on it. The colonel's going to be pleased with me."

Dickinson was the colonel's creature. He had been spying for Howard all along. Cecily felt the white-hot fury that had risen in her when Giles Netherby accosted her in her room.

She bit down on Dickinson's palm, so that he bellowed with pain and loosened his hold on her arm, then eeled out of his grip. When he grabbed for her, she knocked away his hands so hard that his hat flew off.

"You unspeakable swine!" she exclaimed.

With an oath, he leapt at her, and she saw the dull glint of steel in his hand. "When I get me 'ands on you, you'll regret it, me lady," he threatened.

Cecily snatched up a dead branch and parried the footman's knife blows. She knew that Dickinson was much stronger than she and was wondering if she could make a run for the house, when, to her horror, her foot slipped from under her. "Now, me beauty, what'll you do?" Dickinson sneered.

There was a rustle in the underbrush, a movement of shadow, and a click of bone meeting bone, and Dickinson fell like a stone. He lay on the ground and did not move.

"Trevor!" Cecily cried.

He dropped down on one knee and gathered her into his arms. She clung to him stammering, "Thank God I found you, oh, thank God. The colonel is riding for the western downs—"

"I know all about Howard." Swiftly he rose, lifting her with him. "You have no business being out here," he told her. "Go back to the house at once."

Before she could protest, there were halting footsteps, and a tall, shadowy figure came limping up the path toward them. "Ah, good," a cold voice said, "you have stopped the woman."

"She has nothing to do with this business." Though Lord Brandon spoke calmly, Cecily could feel the heightened tension in him. "She is leaving now."

"That she must not do. There is no telling what she has seen. For security's sake, she must be sequestered."

Brandon thrust Cecily behind him. "She's going back to the house."

"No, I am not," Cecily contradicted. "I demand to know who this is."

"Go back to the house, Celia," Lord Brandon said.

"You *know* this hellcat?" There was astonishment in the other man's cold tones.

As though discussing the weather, Lord Brandon replied, "I hope to marry the lady."

There was a silence. Then both Cecily and Cold Voice spoke at once. *"Marry?"* Cecily exclaimed, while the man she had kicked demanded to know if Lord Brandon had taken leave of his senses.

"There's no time for moonshine and madness

now," he said angrily. "You of all people know what the stakes are. What have you confided in this vixen?"

Cecily glared at him. From the very little she could make out of Cold Voice, he looked thoroughly unsavory.

"If I am a vixen," she told him roundly, "you are a rogue. No one but a rogue would accost a female as you did."

There was a little silence, and then Cold Voice said, "Madam, I will offer my apologies at another time. Deal with her, Brandon."

Cecily glared after him as the man limped away. "I am glad I kicked him," she said. "And you are a rogue, too, Lord Brandon, for speaking so scurrilously about marriage."

In spite of himself, Brandon grinned. "Celia, you are beyond price," he said. "You force me to kiss you."

About to protest, Cecily found herself being taken back into his arms and being thoroughly kissed. The kiss lasted for a few seconds only, but in those seconds the sun became unfixed, the world ceased to turn, and night was transformed to brightest day.

For a long moment they stayed fused together, and then Brandon loosed her and stepped away. "Go back to the house now," he told her softly. "Don't worry about me."

She knew that she should do as he said, but she could not bear to see him walk away into danger. "Wait," she temporized. "You do not know that Captain Jermayne has joined the colonel and his Riders. And that Dickinson, here, is the colonel's spy."

"We've had our eye on Master Dickinson for some time." Lord Brandon whistled softly, and two shadows materialized, grasped the unconscious Dickinson by his boot heels, and dragged him away.

"What are you going to do with him?" Cecily wondered nervously.

"He deserves hanging for putting his hands on you, but at least I have broken his nose and his jaw." There was grim satisfaction in Brandon's voice. "Once this is over, he will be set free. Now do what you're asked for once in your life and go back to the house."

He turned on his heel and melted away into the darkness, and there was nothing she could do but to return to Marcham Place, where she found Lady Marcham reading a book in the periwinkle room. Her aunt looked up as she entered and remarked, "Ah, my dear. I wondered where you had got to."

Cecily saw no reason to lie. "I was in the woods, Aunt Emerald. There I was accosted by a tall man with the coldest voice I have ever heard." As she recounted the rest of her adventures, Lady Marcham frankly stared.

"You kicked this icy-voiced knave in the shin, did you say? How extraordinary! Cecily, I begin to have great hopes for you. You will go far."

Cecily had been watching her grandaunt's face closely. "Do you know who the man is?" she asked.

"How could I, when I was not even there?" Lady Marcham asked. "As for Dickinson, I will not peel eggs with you. I had my doubts about him all along. I am sorry for Mary, however, for it is not her fault that her swain is such a thatch-gallows."

With this she returned to her book. Cecily wondered how Aunt Emerald could be so calm. She herself felt as if she were resting on a bed of nails.

The minutes crawled by into hours, and the house began to prepare for sleep. The senior footman had just taken up the candelabra to light the ladies to their beds when Cecily started. "Listen," she whispered, "hoofbeats! Do you think—"

"Colonel Howard is the outside of enough," Lady Marcham exclaimed irritably. "The man has no sense of propriety to come here at such an hour. Well, I suppose I must receive him, but you need not. Go to bed, my dear."

Her voice was as calm as ever, but when Cecily looked into her eyes, she could for once read her grandaunt's thoughts. She went to her and put her arm around the older woman's waist. "We will meet the colonel together," she said.

"Did I not say that you would go far?" Lady Marcham asked affectionately. "Announce the colonel when he arrives, Grigg."

But when the knock came at the door, the voice Cecily heard was not the booming tones of the colonel, and a moment later James Montworthy strutted into the room. He was booted, spurred, armed with sword and pistols, and followed at a respectful distance by half a dozen of the rank and file.

He looked thoroughly pleased with himself as he made his bow and exclaimed, "Glad to see that you ladies are both in plump current, give you m'word on it."

Cecily turned her back. Lady Marcham said coldly, "We thought that you had ridden off with Colonel Howard."

"Truth is, now that Brandon's been exposed as the ringleader of the smugglers—beg your pardon, Lady Marcham, but I'm not one to wrap plain facts in clean linen—I was sure he'd go to earth. So I told the colonel, and he sent me out here with some of the men. Ain't safe for you ladies to be on your own, give you m'word on it."

"Do you stand there and tell me that we are in

danger from my godson?" Lady Marcham demanded impatiently.

"Well, he is a desperate character, ain't he?" Montworthy checked himself and added in a somewhat sheepish tone, "Fact is, Colonel Howard sent me to ... to, ah, search the house and grounds."

Whirling to face him, Cecily cried, "That is beyond everything. Next you will say that Aunt Emerald and I are criminals."

James looked obstinate. "Well, after all, the man *lives* here."

He paused and stared meaningfully at Lady Marcham, who shrugged. "Do as you will, but remember that those who seek often find more than they bargain for. Indeed, you are brave men to search *my* house."

Behind Montworthy the rank and file shifted uneasily, and Cecily heard one of them muttering a charm against magic. "Maybe, unner the circumstances, sorr," one of them ventured to say, "it's best if we just search the grounds, like."

"You'll search what I tell you to," James snapped. "Start below stairs, and do a good job of it. The lower classes," he added loftily as his henchmen clomped away, "try my patience, give you m'word on it. Never use their brain boxes. *Now* what is it?"

One of his retainers had shuffled back into the periwinkle room. "If you please, sorr," he stammered, "If you was to come below stairs—"

"Hoy!" James started like a hound who has scented game. "So Brandon *is* here."

He strode out of the room and down the hall, and Cecily, after a glance at Lady Marcham, ran after him. At the top of the steps that led to the servants' domain, she stopped. James and his followers were standing at the kitchen door.

The door was ajar, and through it wafted the sound of a male voice. Cecily readied herself to shout a warning, but before she could do so, the voice said distinctly, "Is this the right way? Has one got the right touch at last?"

"Sir Carolus?" Cecily wondered. She turned amazed eyes to Montworthy, who had turned brick red.

"Yes, yes!" Mrs. Horris's voice cooed. "You are doing hit so lovely, sir. Keep at hit, keep at hit!"

Sir Carolus and *Mrs. Horris*? It boggled the imagination. James gritted, "That's why he's been acting so odd. I see it now. Smiling to himself, as though he's come into a honeyfall. Looking guilty whenever I chanced on him. Lying to me about his gout tonight so he could sneak over here and . . . and canoodle with a *cook*! How could he do this to me?"

"Ooh, lovely! You got it hup so well," Mrs. Horris moaned. "It's going ter *'old* this time."

James seized his hair with both hands.

"Now?" panted Sir Carolus. "Now?"

With a muffled roar, James burst into the kitchen, then stopped dead in his tracks. The rank and file, who had raced in after their leader, collided with his broad back and stopped also.

Mrs. Horris screamed, and Sir Carolus shouted, "No! You must not—oh, it is too late."

Cecily pushed her way into the kitchen and saw Sir Carolus staring mournfully at a collapsing soufflé. "It had such a beautiful height to it." He sighed. Then, glaring at his son, he added, "How dare you burst in here and ruin my work of art? Why are you here?"

"What are *you* doing here?" James retorted. "Left you in your bed. Said you had gout and was in too much pain for fireworks. You lied to me—"

"If one had told the truth, one would not have had any peace." Sir Carolus looked ready to weep as he put his wilted soufflé down on the table. "It *was* to be a dish of eggs and potatoes and onions with just a kiss of herbs. It was Mrs. Horris's recipe, and she was teaching it to me."

James opened his mouth to speak, but Mrs. Horris had finally recovered her voice. "Isn't a woman safe in her own kitchen?" she shouted. Then, waving her rolling pin, she advanced on the rank and file. "Out, you lot," she threatened. "You hain't wanted in 'ere!"

The colonel's homespun warriors retreated hastily into the hall, from which one of them called, "Shall us search the rest of the 'ouse, sorr?"

Montworthy nodded. He seemed to be beyond speech.

"And you, too, may take yourself off." Sir Carolus shook a finger under his tall son's nose as he added, "Your conduct, sir, is reprehensible in the extreme. What is it to you if one enjoys the culinary arts? From henceforth one intends to cook at Montworthy House."

Obviously taken aback by his sire's vehemence, James swallowed hard and faltered, "But our cook'll give notice, Pater."

"Then let him," announced Sir Carolus. "There are other cooks. Remember that *you* do not own Montworthy House, sir, and that if you are bored in Dorset, you have only your profligate ways to thank. Mend your manners, or you will be in the soup!"

One of the rank and file now peered around the door to report, "Sorr, Lord Brandon ain't in the 'ouse."

With obvious relief James turned away from his outraged sire. "We'll search the woods, then."

His retainer gaped. "The 'Aunted Woods?"

"Where the Widow is supposed to walk at the dark of the moon," Cecily added promptly. "Besides, how can Lord Brandon be in the woods, when he was seen riding toward the western downs?"

But James repeated, "He's in the woods, I tell you. Hoy, Ableman, Pruett—time to draw the coverts. Get lamps and follow me."

Accompanied by his nervous retainers, he clattered up the stairs and out the front door. "What is this about Lord Brandon?" Sir Carolus wondered, but Cecily had no time for explanations. She fairly ran to keep up with Montworthy and the others and found them making their way through the herb garden toward the edge of the woods.

"Hoy," James exclaimed. "Look at that!"

Cecily's heart sank as she saw that Montworthy was pointing to the hat she had knocked off Dickinson's head. It was lying on the edge of the wood, and the light of the lamps picked it out clearly.

Montworthy picked up the hat and examined it. "This is a footman's hat," he said, "and it ain't been lying here long, or it'd be wet with dew. That Dickinson fellow was set up by the colonel to watch out for Brandon. He must've found smugglers inside those woods."

"I collect that you are now a detective." But Cecily's sarcasm was wasted.

His face shining with renewed excitement, Montworthy drew his sword and waved it in the air. "After them, men!" he trumpeted. "The colonel expects us to do our duty."

He plunged through the trees, followed by the rank and file. Cecily, running to catch up, said stoutly, "Cannot you see that this path ends in a solid wall of alders?"

Frowning, James gave one of the bogus trees a

shake, but it had been planted solidly. "You see how ridiculous this all is?" Cecily cried.

"Now that is very odd."

Sir Carolus had followed them into the woods. He was breathing hard from the exertion of keeping up with the others, and while he mopped his forehead with his handkerchief, he stared at the false hedge.

"One remembers these woods well," he said. "One used to play here with poor Marcham when we were both still in leading strings. In those days, the path did not end here."

"That was a long time ago," Cecily said hastily. She was grateful that James was paying no attention to what Sir Carolus had said but was stamping about the woods and stabbing between the alders with his sword.

"The way one remembers it, the path led past the groundkeeper's cottage toward the sea road," the little squire mused. "It is not a road that many used even then, and now few know its existence. One recollects that the road leads from the woods to the Widow's Rock. It was a shortcut, one might say."

"You may have something there, Pater." Montworthy stopped stabbing with his sword, and, striding over to the bogus hedge, gave one of the trees a vicious shake. This time it moved in his hand.

"Hoy," the delighted James exclaimed. "This one don't have roots. Now we're getting to the truth."

"What truth are you talkin' about?" a lazy voice wondered.

Chapter Eleven

Lord Brandon was standing a few feet from them. The lamps held by Montworthy's followers shadowed his eyes so that his expression was unreadable as he strolled toward them saying, "Good evenin', Miss Verving. Sir Carolus, your servant. Back from the colonel's, I see, Montworthy. Got tired of fireworks, did you?"

James snapped, "You're coming with us, Brandon."

Lord Brandon lifted his eyebrows. "Not very mannerly, are you?" he drawled. "However, I'll try not to take offense. It *is* late, so I don't mind goin' back to the house."

Montworthy made a rude noise and said, "I'm taking you to the colonel."

"Now, why would I want to be goin' back to Howard's?" Lord Brandon turned his back on James and addressed Sir Carolus. "I'm glad to see you're feelin' more the thing, sir. How's the gout?"

"Enough of this nattering. I'm arresting you for smuggling." James strode forward and grasped

Brandon's shoulder, but his quarry twisted away. Next moment, Montworthy was lying on his back.

"Rag-mannered young fool," Lord Brandon observed. He flicked dust from his sleeve adding, "You're lucky, Montworthy. If you'd ruined my coat, there'd have been the devil of a dustup."

Montworthy jumped to his feet, clenched his hands, and once again advanced on the duke's son. "You need to be taught a lesson," he vowed. "Come on, damn you. I'll teach you to mock me."

Looking eminently bored, Lord Brandon drew out his snuffbox. With an oath Montworthy knocked the box aside. "You smatterer, will you attend to me?" he shouted.

In that moment Lord Brandon moved. So swiftly that Cecily saw little more than a blur of speed, he struck James a clean, hard blow on his chin. Sir Carolus stared as his son and heir buckled at the knees, then pitched facedown onto the grass.

Cecily knelt at Montworthy's side and felt for a pulse. "He is unconscious," she exclaimed.

She looked up at Lord Brandon, who was rubbing the knuckles of his right hand. "I regret subjectin' a lady to such a sight," he said. "My apologies. And to you also, Sir Carolus."

The little squire trundled forward, bent down, and with an effort turned his offspring on his back. He examined James's jaw and shook his head. "That was a flush hit, Lord Brandon. One has not seen such a whisty castor since one's days at Oxford." He sighed deeply. "I regret to say that James requires knocking down from time to time. One has failed to do one's duty in that respect, one is sorry to say." He looked up earnestly and added, "But I beg you will forgive that nonsense about his arresting you. He is not a bad boy, but unfortunately wanting in the upper works."

As he spoke, there was a low whistle nearby, and the shadowy form of a man slid out of the woods. James's followers, who had gathered awestruck around their leader's felled form, looked up and confronted the muzzle of Lord Brandon's pistol.

"Stay where you are," he ordered. Then, as the newcomer whispered a message, he nodded. "See to it."

As Lord Brandon's man slipped back into the woods, Cecily heard a new sound carried on the wind. "A rider?" she questioned.

"The colonel's Riders," Lord Brandon amended. "They'll be here soon."

He did not seem in the least perturbed, Cecily noted, but the colonel's tenantry took heart. "Now see 'ere, sorr," their leader began, "you 'ad better put that pistol down, or it will go 'ard with you."

Ignoring him, Lord Brandon spoke to Sir Carolus. "Will you escort Miss Vervain back to the house, sir?"

"I shall stay here," Cecily declared.

At that moment there was a chorus of yells in the near distance. "Oh, by Jove," a familiar voice shouted, "the brute's gone mad."

"That is Captain Jermayne," Sir Carolus exclaimed.

There was a crashing, a neighing and whinnying, and the colonel's furious voice. Next moment, a frenzied horse came galloping up the pathway toward them.

"'Ware horse," Captain Jermayne shouted. "I can't control him—out of my way!"

The colonel's retainers threw honor to the winds and ran for their lives. Cecily seized James Montworthy's arms and tried to drag him to safety.

"Shoo, avaunt—get away!" With some idea of protecting his unconscious son, Sir Carolus waved his plump arms at the approaching horse. Surprisingly, it obeyed and stopped dead in its tracks.

"That's that," Captain Jermayne exclaimed in a matter-of-fact voice, adding as he slid down from the saddle, "Couldn't keep him away any longer. Get on Cavalier and make a run for it, old fellow. I'll distract them."

Brandon smiled affectionately at his flushed friend. "A heroic effort, but unnecessary, Jermayne. We're ready to welcome the good colonel."

Clasping his hands behind his back, he assumed his habitual, indolent stance. Even so, Cecily could sense the tension that rippled through his lean, hard-muscled frame.

In spite of her resolve she was suddenly afraid. Cecily searched Lord Brandon's face and saw him mouth the words, "Easy, Celia."

She did not feel at all easy. The woods had begun to echo with the stamp of booted feet and the crackle of branches broken by impatient men. A few more minutes, and the colonel strode into the clearing.

"So!" he exclaimed.

Followed by a dozen of his Riders and many more of the rank and file, Colonel Howard strode into the clearing. Like Caesar at the head of his legions, he looked around to gloat, then saw Captain Jermayne. "You!" he exclaimed in tones of loathing. "If you had been under my command, I would have seen you cashiered."

The captain protested, "It wasn't my fault that my horse bolted. By Jove, no. The brute ran off with me. And was it *my* fault that you were in my way?" He paused to add solicitously, "Hope you weren't hurt too much by being knocked on your—hem!— out of the saddle."

With a final glare at Jermayne the colonel transferred his attention to the duke's son. "Well, well,

well," he sneered. "So the fox has been run to earth."

Sir Carolus protested, "Colonel, there is no need to take that tone. Lord Brandon—"

"Lord Brandon is a smuggler." The colonel all but smacked his lips as he said the word. "You did not expect to see me here, did you, Brandon? You thought I would be on my way to the western downs chasing wagons filled with rubbish. I tell you, you'll catch cold trying to gammon *me*. I smelled a rat straightaway."

"Did you?" Lord Brandon murmured.

"You thought I would follow that red herring and leave you free to move your contraband undeterred. Instead, I sent a dozen of my men *and* the watch to follow Horris, while these gentlemen and I came to arrest you. When Montworthy gives me his report—"

For the first time the colonel became aware of the prostrate James. He frowned. "Is he dead?" he demanded.

Sir Carolus shook his head, and the rank and file, who had ventured out of their hiding places, began to explain at once. "Silence!" the colonel ordered. "That can wait. Seize Lord Brandon."

"For what reason and by what authority?" Cecily demanded hotly. "He has done nothing but walk in his godmother's woods. It is *you* who are trespassing."

One of the Riders who had been advancing with the intent of placing Lord Brandon under arrest stopped and looked questioningly at Colonel Howard, who repeated, "Arrest him at once."

"How dare you, sir!"

Lady Marcham's clear voice startled them all. Even Brandon looked astonished as his godmother, followed by her servants, glided into the clearing.

"How dare you put your hands on Lord Brandon?" the lady repeated.

Lady Marcham was still dressed in her party clothes. With her rich pelisse flung about her shoulders and a scarf of some silvery gauze crowning her hair, she looked regal. Offended dignity seemed to add inches to her height, and the eyes she fixed on the colonel glittered like frozen jade.

"If I understood you correctly," Lady Marcham continued, "you ordered my godson's arrest. It is beyond everything that you dare to trespass on my land and issue such an order."

Colonel Howard looked taken aback for a moment, but then he rallied. After all, Lady Marcham was but a woman, and no mere female could come between him and justice.

"The man is a smuggler," he retorted.

"So *you* say," Lord Brandon murmured.

"Actually," Captain Jermayne interposed, "I'd like to see some proof. No joke accusing a duke's son. No, by Jove."

A mutter of agreement began to circulate among the rank and file, and one of the Riders cleared his throat. "You *do* have proof, don't you sir? I mean, about Lord Brandon's involvement—"

As if his words were a signal, Lady Marcham's servants began to talk at once. The motherly housekeeper insisted that Master Trevor was as blameless as a day-old lamb. The senior footman pleaded for his lordship's release. The pot boy began to blubber. Mrs. Horris was heard to insist that Colonel Howard was as mad as a March hare for even suggesting that Lord Brandon had done anything wrong.

"The man is a common criminal!" the colonel roared above the babble. "He has broken the law."

His lip rose in a sneer. "Perhaps, Lady Marcham, you are his accomplice."

Brandon's head snapped up. "You will not speak to Lady Marcham in this way," he began, but his godmother gestured him quiet. "Are you accusing *me*, sirrah?" she demanded.

Even the colonel quailed before that tone and that look. "Since you defend the criminal—" he began uneasily.

"You are the criminal, sirrah!" Lady Marcham hissed. "You dare set foot on my land. You dare to come into these woods. Be careful, Colonel Howard. Remember where you are."

It almost seemed to Cecily that as Lady Marcham spoke, she grew in stature. There was a whimper of fear from among her staff, and Cecily saw Mary cowering behind Mrs. Horris.

"We're in the Haunted Woods, that's where," Mary quavered, "at the dark of the moon. Holy saints preserve us now at the hour of our death."

Cecily noted that the colonel's tenants had begun to edge back along the path. Apparently the colonel had seen this, too, for he said contemptuously, "Are you old women that you're afraid of hobgoblins? Stop mucking about. Seize that man!"

Obediently a Rider stepped forward. As he did so, Lady Marcham flung wide her arms in a dramatic gesture that caught him in the face. He staggered back clutching his nose as she declaimed, "There are forces, dark and old, that you defy in these woods. Hush! Can you not hear their age-old voices in the wind?"

Cecily found herself holding her breath and listening with the others. It seemed as though the woods had definitely acquired a voice. Not of haunts and goblins but of ancient truths and knowledge that had existed when England was still young.

But the colonel was not impressed. "Lady Marcham, I beg you'll return to the house. You too, Miss Vervain."

"I do not take orders from you," Cecily snapped.

Out of patience, the colonel grasped Cecily's arm. "I *said* that you were to leave," he gritted.

That was as far as he got before Lord Brandon hurled himself across the glade and choked the words back into his throat. Colonel Howard tried to defend himself, but he could do nothing against hands that tightened like steel bands around his neck. His eyes nearly popped out of his skull, and he gasped and gargled for air.

"I say, old boy, don't kill him," Captain Jermayne exclaimed. "He's Miss Howard's father."

The captain's judicious voice recalled Brandon to sanity. He shoved the colonel away from him, so that he fell on his knees beside the prone Montworthy.

"You'll meet me for this," Howard panted. "You'll meet me now, with swords."

On the point of replying that there was nothing he would like better, Brandon checked himself. Dueling with the colonel was not a part of his plan. He should never have lost his control, but when the man had laid his hand on Cecily—

For a second Lord Brandon hesitated. Then he turned his back. " 'Pon my honor," he drawled, "I'll not duel with you tonight, Howard. Another time, perhaps."

"Now!" The colonel got to his feet and drew his sword. "Now, or I'll run you through for a craven dog."

"Here, old boy, take this." Eyes hard, Captain Jermayne unsheathed his own sword and extended it to Lord Brandon. "Can't let any man alive call you a coward. No, by Jove."

"Oh, Trevor."

Cecily had spoken in a whisper, but Brandon's eyes went to her at once. His mind was filled with conflicting emotions. He had not wanted this combat, and yet now that it had been thrust upon him, something cold and watchful in him welcomed it. A man like the colonel would never be satisfied until he had ferreted out events and secrets that must not be revealed. It was best to kill him, make an end.

"Coward," grated the colonel. "I'll expose you, by God. I'll tell the world about tonight."

With his face hard and set, Brandon asked, "You'll act for me, Jermayne?"

"Greatest pleasure in the world, Brandon."

"Sir Carolus?" The little squire nodded resolutely. "In that case, I await your pleasure, colonel."

Some of the Riders were expostulating with their chief, but the colonel shrugged such counsel aside. "Farmington, Rogerford—you'll act for me? Now, gentlemen, make a ring around us and hold the lamps high. We need light."

Obediently the colonel's followers fanned out to make a living circle in the clearing. Brandon paid them no attention but watched Cecily instead. Even in the ruddy lamplight she had gone pale, and there was a growing horror in her eyes.

"I will escort the ladies to the house and be back at once," Sir Carolus said, but Lady Marcham shook her head.

"I am staying also," Cecily said resolutely.

Without another word Brandon strode forward into the human circle and faced the colonel. Howard was taller, with longer arms. He himself was younger, quicker. Black eyes and blue locked.

"En garde," Brandon said.

Cecily wanted to cry out in protest, but she could not speak. Perhaps her blood had turned to ice, for she felt heavy and cold. She started as a hand clasped her shoulder, then realized that Lady Marcham had come to stand beside her. "Steady, my dear," her grandaunt murmured.

No one else said anything. There was no sound but hard breathing and the metallic rasp of steel sliding against steel. Then the colonel lunged forward. All the brutal power of the man was in that blow, but it glanced harmlessly off Lord Brandon's blade. As he easily beat back the colonel's attack, Cecily realized that the duke's son was a swordsman that few could match.

Feint, parry, and then a lightning double thrust—a sigh ran about the living circle as blood spurted from the colonel's arm. Black in the lamplight, it dripped down his sleeve.

The duelists circled again. As the lamplight fell on Brandon's set face, Cecily clutched Lady Marcham's hand. "Aunt Emerald, he means to kill the colonel."

"It will fall as it will fall," Lady Marcham replied. Her soft voice was as inflexible as her godson's eyes.

"But if he kills the colonel, Trevor will have to leave England," Cecily mourned.

Within the circle Brandon was thinking that if he felled Howard, he would be facing worse things than exile. Even if she understood and realized that this was the only possible course of action, she would never forget that he had once killed a man in front of her. The colonel's blood would lie between them forever.

But, he reasoned unhappily, not to kill the man would have worse consequences. What he had committed himself to do weighed more heavily in the scales than individual happiness. He had only one choice, even though that choice might be one he would regret forever.

Through crossed blades, Lord Brandon glanced at Cecily, and the unhappiness in his eyes went to her heart. Unable to watch any more, she closed her eyes.

At that moment, a cold, inflexible voice spoke. "Put up your swords," it ordered. "Put them up *now*."

Cecily's eyes flew open. She looked toward the false thicket of alders and saw there a man with a face like a hawk. He was tall and powerfully built, and his eyes were dark and piercing. A high-bridged nose shadowed an arrogant mouth.

"Good heavens," Sir Carolus cried, "it's the Duke of Pershing!"

"The Duke of *Pershing*?" Cecily gasped.

The duke did not even glance at her. His attention was riveted on the combatants, neither of whom had lowered his blade. "This must cease," he said sternly. "Inquiries into a duel will lead to trouble later on. Brandon, do you hear me? Remember that we act for the good of our country."

Limping slightly, he stepped between the combatants and with his walking stick forced their blades apart. Colonel Howard snarled, "So you are in this as well, your grace. I cannot credit that you are a criminal like your son."

"Hold your tongue, sir," the duke commanded. He indicated James. "Is he dead?"

Sir Carolus began a long-winded explanation but was cut short by the duke, who demanded, "Who the devil are you?"

With a curious kind of dignity, the little squire replied, "One is named Sir Carolus Montworthy, your grace. The young man on the ground is one's son, James. Members of our family have had the privilege of fighting for England many times through the years. One does not understand what all this means, but one would gladly sacrifice one's life in England's service."

The duke nodded, then turned to Cecily. "And you, madam?" he asked, curtly.

"This is Miss Cecily Vervain, sir," Brandon explained, "Lady Marcham's grandniece." As Cecily curtsied, he added, "I think you have made her acquaintance."

"The lady has made a definite impact on me, yes."

His voice was hard, dry, colder than ever. Some instinct warned Cecily that if she quailed before the Duke of Pershing now, he would forever hold her in contempt. It took all of her courage to meet his black gaze, but she did so.

"Our first meeting was indeed memorable, your grace," she said.

A strong forefinger extended itself, tucked itself under Cecily's chin and lifted it. Perhaps it was a trick of the moonlight, but the duke's eyes now no longer appeared quite so cold. In fact, his thin, aristocratic lips actually twitched at the corners as he commented, "So you are related to Lady Marcham. You don't have her looks, but you do have her spirit."

"Thank you, your grace," Cecily murmured.

For a moment the duke looked almost human. Then the colonel exclaimed, "Pershing's arrival does not change things. I came to arrest you, Brandon, for smuggling, and I mean to do so."

He gestured his staring retainers forward, but Lord Brandon said, "If you look about you, you'll see that you're outnumbered."

Cecily looked about her with the others and noted

that a contingent of men had materialized out of the trees. They were all armed and had their weapons trained on the colonel and his followers.

"Put down your weapons," Brandon ordered.

The colonel had gone as white as the handkerchief he had tied around his wound. "Your smuggler band?" he sneered.

"There are no smugglers except in your head," Lord Brandon said impatiently. "These men are law-abiding Englishmen."

"All the time you thought you had Brandon trapped, he had you trapped," Captain Jermayne exclaimed. "Funny, that. By Jove, yes."

"You won't be harmed," Brandon went on. "You'll be detained for a time and then released. Then you'll return to your homes."

"The devil I will!" the colonel spluttered. "I will see you in hell first."

He got no further, for now into the lamplit glade walked a tall, thin figure dressed in diaphanous white. Her long fair hair was unbound, and moonlight teased it into an eerie nimbus. She walked hesitantly, looking from side to side as though searching for something—or someone.

Mary fell to her knees and began to cross herself violently. "Holy saints, shield us," she wailed. "It's the Widow's ghost! It's herself, come to take one of us to the other world with her!"

Chapter Twelve

The sepulchral figure raised its head hopefully and quavered, "Is that you, Mary?"

Mary's eyes were as huge as saucers. "Not me," she wailed. "I won't go with you."

Just then James Montworthy sat up and blinked at the figure in white. He gaped. "What in hell—"

"Aye, it comes from hell. It's the Widow's ghost," Mary keened.

James's jaw was aching, his head was pounding like the devil's own anvil, and his ears were ringing. There seemed to be a mist before his eyes. The slow-returning memory of being planted a facer by Brandon rankled. It was the last straw to be confronted by a smuggler dressed up as a ghost.

Drawing his pistol, he threatened, "You in white! Stop or I'll shoot."

Brandon started forward, but Captain Jermayne was swifter. He threw himself between Montworthy's pistol and the white figure. Cecily cried, "No! Do not shoot—it is Delinda!"

As her anguished cry echoed through the woods, a second apparition burst onto the scene. Montworthy dropped his pistol and yelled in pain as Archimedes sank his twenty claws and one tooth into his right arm.

"It's that witch cat! Run for your lives!" Mrs. Horris shouted.

She hitched up her skirts and fled but was soon outpaced by Mary. All of Lady Marcham's servants save Grigg followed, and after that, it was every man for himself. The colonel's orders and threats could not stop the stampede as his rank and file fairly knocked each other down in their haste to get away. There was a pounding of feet, shouts, curses, and a thudding of frenzied hooves receding into the distance.

Finally there was silence. Brandon's forces closed in about the colonel's depleted band while their leader walked across to James, caught Archimedes by the scruff of the neck, and pried him loose.

"Are you all right, Miss Howard?" Captain Jermayne was asking anxiously.

"I do not know—I am so frightened. Why are you all here in Lady Marcham's woods?" Delinda stammered.

"What are *you* doing here?" the colonel thundered.

Blanching visibly, Delinda hung her head and murmured, "I was only looking for verbena."

Brandon carried Archimedes over to Cecily, deposited him in her arms, and whispered, "Is that girl touched in the head?"

"You are mad," the colonel shouted. "I will have you packed away to a madhouse."

Threateningly he advanced on Delinda, but once again Captain Jermayne stepped between her and peril. "Wouldn't do to do violence to a lady," he said mildly.

Colonel Howard grasped Captain Jermayne's shoulder, but the younger officer refused to budge.

"The thing to do is calm down and think it over," he soothed.

"I agree," Pershing said. "Your army seems to have diminished, Howard. What do you say now?"

"You think that because we are outnumbered, we will surrender to you?" Contempt hardened the colonel's voice. "I would never dishonor myself by giving in to brigands."

The duke looked impatiently at the colonel and at his Riders, who had ranged themselves behind their chief.

"I am growing weary of this," he declared. "All of you must leave at once. I want your word that you will not speak of this night to anyone."

"One is more than happy to comply," Sir Carolus chirruped, but his son growled, "Not so fast, Pater. The duke is trying to cover up for his precious son, but it won't fadge. Something havey-cavey is going on. Mean to know what, give you m'word."

He got shakily to his feet, rubbed his jaw, and glared at Lord Brandon, who told the duke, "You'll have to silence them one way or another, sir."

There was an ominous pause during which Sir Carolus looked alarmed, the ladies drew closer together, and the colonel and his followers assumed martial poses. At last the duke barked, "I have no choice but to take you into my confidence, but what I am about to say to you must never be divulged to anyone. Not three hundred yards away—"

"Is a band of cursed smugglers. I knew it!"

The duke leveled a withering look on the colonel. "Not three hundred yards away a meeting is being held to end the war between England and America."

There was a stunned silence. Then Sir Carolus

stammered, "But—but are the peace talks not at Ghent?"

"On August nineteenth, those talks became hopelessly deadlocked. The Americans were ready to break off negotiations. To forestall an escalation of the war, a plan was devised."

Negotiations were undertaken, Pershing said, to invite an American of high rank and honor to England. Here the American delegate would meet with an Englishman of equivalent rank. Between them, it was hoped, they could come to agreements that would then be taken back to the conference table.

"Do you expect me to believe that?" Colonel Howard sneered. "The Americans would never risk sending their man to England."

"There were risks on both sides. We had much to lose in allowing foreign ships to lay anchor off the English coast." The duke paused. "Also, we had to maintain complete secrecy. Had they known, those in our government opposed to peace would have tried desperate measures to prevent the talks."

The colonel looked as though he were about to speak again, but Pershing snapped, "Be silent and do not interrupt me further! The rest is simply told. We chose Dorset as a site for the meeting because Lady Marcham's late husband was once acquainted with the family of—of the American delegate. And Lady Marcham's family have also been for years the trusted friends of the gentleman chosen to represent England."

The duke's fierce eyes softened as he bowed to Lady Marcham. "Lady Marcham is a gallant woman," he said. "She knew there would be danger in agreeing to allow this meeting to take place on her estate, but she accepted the risk. It was her suggestion that the meeting be held in her woods.

She reasoned that her own, er, reputation and the locals' fear of the Haunted Woods would keep people away."

The colonel's Riders looked impressed at this, and Sir Carolus nodded his head several times. "One admits that it makes sense. But, your grace, where does Lord Brandon fit into all of this?"

"My duty was to coordinate security for the meeting." Crisply Lord Brandon continued, "As Lady M.'s godson, I had an excuse for a prolonged visit to Dorset. I know the waters hereabouts and could guide the Americans to make landfall at the most unlikely spot possible. Unfortunately I didn't foresee that Colonel Howard would be a neighbor."

The colonel muttered something beneath his breath. "His obsession with smugglers made him ready to suspect any stranger," Brandon continued. "So I had to play the fool."

"You did it exceedingly well," Captain Jermayne exclaimed. "A proper cake you made of yourself."

"I had been away at the wars, so people put the change in me down to war experiences." Lord Brandon smiled at Cicely. "Most people dismissed me as a fribble."

Montworthy burst out, "You mean to tell me that *you* planned this meeting? Next you'll say that *all* the smugglers are working for the crown."

"Of course they are. These gentlemen served with me on the Peninsula. Others, like Cully Horris, were boyhood friends. Among the servants Grigg was aware of what was happening, and my valet is even now leading a convoy of empty wagons toward the downs."

"And of course I guessed," Captain Jermayne cut in. "I mean to say, a man decorated three times for valor on the Peninsula, a man who saved my life— not likely to become a counter-coxcomb, is he?"

As Cecily listened, it was as though a complicated tapestry pattern was at last taking shape. Montworthy apparently thought so, too, for he said in an aggrieved tone, "I suppose you think I owe you an apology for the things I said. You won't get it, give you m'word on't."

"Apology be hanged!" the colonel rumbled. "I do not believe a word of what you have said, your grace. Who is this so-called English delegate? You?"

The duke strode over to the colonel, and Cecily held her breath. But instead of challenging him to a duel for doubting his word, the tall peer merely said, "Come walk with me, and you will have your answer."

The colonel started to gesture his Riders forward, but the duke raised an imperious hand. "You will come alone, colonel."

"Might be a trap," James suggested. He then encountered Brandon's hard stare and fell silent.

Momentarily the colonel hesitated. Then he said, "I will see this business through. You gentlemen stay here."

Together the duke and Colonel Howard disappeared through the alders. "I do not understand anything," Delinda said, sighing.

With a smile Lord Brandon turned to her. "Never mind, ma'am. You've done very well. But why were you in Lady M.'s woods at this time of night?"

Delinda looked flustered. "I was here to gather some herbs. I heard voices—I nearly ran away—and then I recognized Papa's voice, so I came to see what was happening." She took a deep breath, then asked plaintively, "Why was Mr. Montworthy about to shoot me?"

"I suspect that he thought you were a smuggler," Cecily explained.

"I still do not understand." Sadly Delinda looked

at James, who was engaged in wiping mud off his coat. "I did not find any verbena, Cecily. Perhaps it was not to be."

Captain Jermayne cleared his throat. "I think you were splendid, Miss Howard."

"You do?"

The captain started to speak, blushed, and glanced at Cecily for support. "Absolutely right," he resumed. "When you came into the glade pretending to be the ghost, I nearly applauded. You did it so well."

Delinda blinked and looked at Captain Jermayne as though she were waking from a deep sleep.

"You came at just the right time. You averted a confrontation. And looked so beautiful. Your hair was like—like a cloud of gold."

Delinda's blush was visible even by lamplight, but her eyes were bright. "It was you who was brave," she breathed. "Oh, Captain Jermayne, you could have been *killed.*"

"For you I would gladly lay down my life. Anytime." The captain would have said more, but his shyness caught up with him. He attempted to continue, stammered, and got hopelessly tongue-tied.

Cecily came to the rescue. "It has become very cool," she said. "Do you not think so, Captain Jermayne? I collect that it will be warmer at Marcham Place."

She looked significantly at the captain, who exclaimed, "Eh? By Jove, yes, you're right. Permit me, Miss Howard, to escort you back to the house."

Delinda's lips curved into a tremulous smile. As she took the captain's proffered arm and walked away with him, Brandon remarked to Cecily, "Exeunt newfound sweethearts."

"I think they will suit famously. Delinda is a dear, and Captain Jermayne is a kind person. And a good friend, too—only think of his pretending to be carried away by his horse so that you would have time to escape the colonel."

She broke off as the duke came striding back through the alders. The colonel followed, and Cecily was startled at the change in him. His bombast was gone, he looked ten years older, and he walked as though he were in a dream.

"Obviously you told him," Brandon said, and the duke nodded.

Turning to the colonel he then ordered, "Howard, do your duty!"

The colonel wiped his damp forehead, then spoke in a voice hoarse with emotion. "I swear," he said, "that I will never reveal what I have learned this night. Torture will not pry a single word from my lips. As a loyal Englishman and a gentleman, I have sworn it."

He turned to his staring followers. "Gentlemen, I require the same oath from you. Whatever you have seen tonight, you will forget. You will never utter a word about this matter again, even among yourselves."

Astounded but impressed, all the Riders swore silence. The colonel now saluted the duke. "We are at your disposal, your grace," he said.

"Are you so?" The duke's thin lips twitched into an ironic smile. "In that case—Brandon, what orders do you have for the colonel?"

"Hoy, see here—" bleated Montworthy, but no one paid attention to him.

The colonel seemed to be struggling with himself. Then, with the air of one who intends to face a firing squad with dignity, he wheeled about on his boot heels and glared at Lord Brandon. "Sir, your orders?" he barked.

"Guard the sea road together with my men. Divert my travelers until the American ships are safe at sea," Brandon said. Then he added quietly, "We haven't seen eye to eye in the past, Howard, but in this matter we both serve England."

Wordlessly the colonel saluted the man he had threatened to jail for smuggling. Then, gesturing to his Riders, he strode out of the glade. "Exeunt the reformed Captain Hackum," Brandon murmured.

"Well, Lady Marcham, it seems as if we have carried it off."

The duke had strolled over to Lady Marcham, who said heartily, "We have indeed. La, your grace, I vow that it is kind of you to think that I have not changed through the years, but the world has turned several times since we were young. And you are looking tired. Come back to Marcham Place, and I will give you some elderberry wine."

The duke looked surprised. "I forget that you are an enchantress, Emerald. Unfortunately I must travel with *him* and make sure that he returns to London safely."

The duke inclined his stately head to kiss Lady Marcham's hand, then exclaimed, "The devil! What's this?"

Something rough and hairy was rubbing against his boot, and a rumbling growl permeated the air. "Miss Vervain's cat is purring," Brandon explained. "He's taken a liking to you."

Having apparently reassured himself that the duke was harmless, the cat padded over to Cecily. She bent down to pick him up, but Lady Marcham said, "Leave him, my dear. He has done famously tonight and very probably kept James from shooting Delinda or her nice captain. Archimedes shall follow us back to the house and have a large bowl of milk."

Sir Carolus, who had been standing bemused during the past ten minutes, came to life with a jerk. "Milk," he murmured, "with a little rum, a sprinkle of nutmeg. In short, milk punch. Mrs. Horris can no doubt make a milk punch that will rival the nectar of the gods."

He began to trundle away toward Marcham Place, and Lady Marcham followed. Archimedes ran ahead, his tail waving like a victorious banner.

The Ice Duke watched them go. He then drew a deep breath that might have been a sigh and said, "I must return to the meeting. Miss Vervain, I look forward to our next encounter. Trevor, I leave the rest in your hands."

Lord Brandon gave an order. As his men silently melted into the trees, he said to Cecily, "It is near the end of the play. Come with me and see the curtain fall."

He offered her his arm, and feeling as though she were not quite awake, she took it. They stepped through the false hedge and followed the path until it broadened into the fork in the road. One side of the fork ran toward the woods. Following the other, they arrived at a clearing. In the center of this clearing stood a cottage.

A nasal voice demanded, "Who goes thar?" Brandon gave the proper password and was allowed to approach the cottage. Cecily noted that though smoke poured from the chimney and lamps burned at the windows, the well-guarded doors of the cottage were closed. Obviously, the meeting was still in progress.

One of the men guarding the door now stepped forward and saluted. "Lord Brandon," he said, "may I inquire who this lady is?"

By his voice Cecily recognized the American with whom she had heard Brandon conspire. She looked questioningly at Trevor, who said, "Miss Vervain, I beg to present Major Barnaby Simpson from Boston."

Cecily found herself looking into bright blue eyes that held both admiration and curiosity. "Honored, ma'am," he said. "Permit me to say that you are the fairest thing I've seen for months."

He bowed and went back to his post. "Since he's been at sea for months, that is hardly a compliment," Cecily said, laughing.

"Americans have no sense of style." Brandon guided Cecily into the shadows of the trees that surrounded the cottage, then stopped to say, "Now, Celia, tell me. Do you see why I had to keep my silence?"

He was standing so close to her that she could feel his warm breath on her cheek. Cecily stepped back a few paces before replying, "It would have been so much easier if I had known what you were about."

"But if you had, we would not have grown to know each other so well."

His tone was tender but assured, too, and some note in it seemed to blow the cobwebs and mist away from Cecily's brain. Gravely she looked up at him and said, "I do not know if I really know you."

"How do you mean?"

"I mean that you have been playing a part, Trevor. In real life you are a duke's son. You are respected, and perhaps wealthy, too—"

"Very wealthy," he agreed. "Brandon's a rich estate—what of it?"

"In real life," Cecily repeated, "we are very different in rank and wealth. Ordinarily we would not have become allies." No matter how she attempted to keep her voice steady and serious, she could not help a small quiver from entering it. "You see, I have been playing a part, too."

Lord Brandon said nothing, and the night seemed very still except for the mutter and pound of the sea. "You have said many times that the world is a stage," Cecily continued. "Now the drama is over, and we must go our separate ways."

She started to turn away from him, but he put his hands on her shoulders and held her back. "Celia, what maggot have you taken into your head? You heard me tell my father that I hoped to marry you, didn't you?"

"The duke," she pointed out, "suggested that you had gone mad. I am persuaded that you spoke without thinking, that on reflection you cannot have meant what you said."

"Why? How?" The hands on Cecily's shoulders tightened. "And don't quote what the duke said— speak for yourself. Why do you think I do not really want to marry you?"

She drew a deep breath and prepared to point out, reasonably and logically, that a duke's son and a penniless young woman of no rank could hardly suit. Instead, she heard herself whisper, "Because you have not once told me that you love me."

Brandon heard the catch in her voice, and his own voice was husky as he replied, "No, I haven't. Why need I tell you that I love you when I can't think of life without you? You are my heart of hearts, my sun, my morning light."

The little glade was silent, and in that silence Cecily could hear his breathing and the beat of her own heart. Looking up into his eyes, she said simply, "I love you, Trevor."

"And I love you with all my heart," he replied, "and I most humbly ask for your hand in marriage." His voice held tender humor as he added,

"Your father isn't alive, so I can't ask *him,* and in any case, he would tell you to make up your own mind."

Cecily drew a long, shaky, happy breath. She was so full of joy that she could hardly bear to stand still. Her body as well as her spirit wanted to dance. As seriously as she could, she said, "I shall marry you as soon as I am certain that the duke was wrong and that you are in your right mind."

"In my right—what the devil do you mean?"

"Well, we are standing in a patch of verbena, which Delinda says is used in a love potion—"

"We don't need any damned love potion," Brandon interrupted. "Come here."

Their lips met again, and again there was silence, and in that silence Cecily knew that she had come home at last.

The sound of voices within the cottage interrupted them, and the lovers drew apart reluctantly. Brandon said, "The meeting seems to be over."

The door of the cottage opened, and the sentries saluted smartly as a dozen armed men emerged. They formed a bodyguard for two gentlemen, both of whom were cloaked and muffled to the eyes.

These gentlemen shook hands. Then one of them, together with his entourage, began to walk down the path that led to the Widow's Rock. The other man and his escort—among whom Cecily recognized the commanding figure of the Duke of Pershing—remained where they were.

"What are they all waiting for?" Cecily whispered to Brandon.

There was a rattle of wheels, and a carriage came up the sea road. It stopped beside the cottage, and once again the sentries saluted as the second gentleman began to walk to the carriage.

Stepping forward, Brandon bowed deeply. Cecily

curtsied. The unknown gentleman nodded to them and moved on. As he did so, Cecily heard Pershing say something in a respectful tone.

Wide-eyed, she rounded on Brandon. "Trevor, can it be true? Could that gentleman possibly be—"

His fingers on her lips stopped her words. "No, love," he warned.

"But I distinctly heard the duke call him by his name," Cecily insisted. "Tell me this—am I wrong?"

His face was grave. "No, you are not wrong."

Tightening his arm about her waist, he drew her back into the shadows. From there they watched Pershing escort his companion to the waiting carriage. The carriage, Cecily noted, was a plain one without ornament or crest. The coachman wore black, and the horses, too, were black. If anyone from the village should chance to see this carriage passing through the woods, they would doubtless hide in fear.

"Now I understand how high the stakes were," she murmured. "Oh, Trevor, Trevor, what a weight you have had on your shoulders! If anything had happened to—to *him*, it would have been a disaster for England."

"No one must know he was here." Brandon kissed Cecily again before adding with a flash of his old, foppish drawl, "But heart up, Miss Verving, all is not lost. No doubt he'll come to dance at our wedding."